RECIPES FROM THE WORLD OF TOLKIEN

Volume II

The Elven Cookbook

First published in Great Britain in 2022 by Cassell,
an imprint of Octopus Publishing Group Ltd
Carmelite House
50 Victoria Embankment
London, EC4Y 0DZ
www.octopusbooks.co.uk

An Hachette UK Company
www.hachette.co.uk

The authorized representative in the EEA is Hachette Ireland, 8 Castlecourt Centre, Dublin 15,
D15 XTP3, Ireland (email: info@hbgi.ie)

ISBN: 978-0-7537-3468-1
eISBN: 978-0-7537-3511-4

A CIP catalogue record for this book is available from the British Library

Printed and bound in China

10 9 8 7 6 5 4 3

MIX
Paper | Supporting
responsible forestry
FSC
www.fsc.org   FSC® C008047

Publisher: Lucy Pessell
Designer: Hannah Coughlin
Editor: Sarah Kennedy
Editorial Assistant: Emily Martin
Recipe Development: Jane Birch
Production Managers: Lucy Carter and Nic Jones

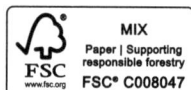

This book has not been prepared, authorized, licensed or endorsed by J.R.R. Tolkien's heirs or estate, nor by any
of the publishers or distributors of the book *The Lord of the Rings* or any other work written by J.R.R. Tolkien,
nor anyone involved in the creation, production or distribution of the films based on the book.

RECIPES FROM THE WORLD OF TOLKIEN

Volume II

The Elven Cookbook

Recipes Inspired by
the Elves of Tolkien

Robert Tuesley Anderson

C CASSELL

Contents

Introduction

We know far less about Tolkien's Elves' eating traditions, customs and meals than his Hobbits' or Men's – there is certainly nothing to compare, in all our encounters with this immortal, otherworldly people, with the blow-by-blow account of the 'unexpected' tea party we are treated to at the start of *The Hobbit*. We do not know how many meals the Elves ate in a day – though we imagine certainly not the five the food-oriented Hobbits aspire to – nor do we get to know what their favourite ingredients or dishes are. Generally, Tolkien keeps his readers' prying eyes away from the Elves' domestic lives, and thereby points up their difference from the other, 'earthier' peoples of Middle-earth. The Elves may be a part of the world, but they somehow live in a different atmosphere.

What is certain is that the Elves do eat and drink, and appear to enjoy doing so. Immortal they may be, but they are subject to hunger, as the Exiles' epic trek across the Grinding Ice in *The Silmarillion* reveals. And they are fond of feasting and merrymaking – there are frequent references to feasts of welcome and celebration in the tales of Beleriand – and from *The Hobbit* we know that the Elvenking of Mirkwood (Thranduil) is more than partial to good red wine, imported in large numbers of barrels from the East. Thranduil, it seems, is as greedy as any Dwarf or Hobbit, and his example, along with those of several other Elves, suggests that they may not quite as ethereal and appetite-less as they might at first appear. The tantalizing glimpse – or should we say smell? – of the roasting faggots and baking bannocks that Bilbo encounters when he first arrives in Rivendell during the Quest of Erebor certainly suggests a more complex picture of Elvish cuisine than the fresh draughts, gathered fruits and vegetables, and sustaining waybreads that otherwise seem to predominate. Elves are certainly not (at least not solely) vegan ascetics.

In both *The Lord of the Rings* and *The Hobbit*, we often feel we are sitting down to dine with the adventurers – tucking into a bowl of buttered mushrooms at Farmer Maggot's kitchen table, cutting into a fragrant blackberry tart at The Prancing Pony in Bree or spooning cream and honey onto bread in the House of Tom Bombadil. We become Frodo's, Sam, Merry's and Pippin's table companions, all the while drawing on our own memories of food to enhance our enjoyment, our savouring, of Tolkien's consummate storytelling.

This is not the case with the Elves – it is hard to imagine sharing a dish of rabbit stew with Lady Galadriel – so one of the primary goals of the following collection of recipes is to fill that gap: to let us dine and make merry with the Elves.

The Eldar – to give the Elves their true name – are by no means a monolithic people – in their characteristics, their languages and their cultures, they are if anything more various than Men (see the diagram on page 9). Tolkien devoted volumes to imagining and developing the Elvish kindreds and their histories – stretching back into the deepest past – and created the vast diversity of landscapes in which they lived – forest, mountain, valleys, sea coast – and the flora and fauna that flourished alongside them. It is to these exhaustive details that we must look if we want more clues about what the Elves ate and drank.

For example, of all Tolkien's kindreds of Elves, the group known as the Teleri are the most closely associated with the sea and seafaring. The evolution of the various kindreds, as described in *The Silmarillion*, are extremely complex: originally the Teleri were the third and most numerous of the houses of the Eldar (Firstborn) that awoke in the far east of Middle-earth and were led by two brothers, Elwë and Olwë. Even in this kindred's earliest days, Tolkien tells us, they began to build rafts, then boats and finally ships to sail on the great inland Sea of Rhûn, so we can imagine that, even at this 'prehistory', they loved to cook the fish that lived in this vast freshwater lake and the rivers and streams that flowed into it. Tolkien subsequently shows how the Teleri's love of Middle-earth's waters grows still deeper when they reach the shores of Beleriand, where they also find a protector in the Maia Ossë, a spirit of the seas. The Vala Ulmo – Tolkien's Poseidon or Neptune of a kind – arrives to take the Teleri across the ocean to Valinor, tethering an island to the shore to act as a ferry and then anchoring the islandferry far out at sea. On this island, Tol Eressëa, the Teleri – now known as the Sea-Elves – live for many years, until, aided by Ossë, they build ships and migrate westwards to Aman, settling on its shores next to their beloved sea. The Teleri must have been expert fishermen as well as shipbuilders, although Tolkien is silent on this matter. We can well imagine the Teleri swan-ships bringing home vast catches of fish, lobsters and other seafoods to the port-city of Alqualondë, to feed the kindred's burgeoning population, as well as the gathering of seaweeds, mussels and other fruits of the shores and inlets as they sought to add still further variety and interest to the Teleri's pescatarian cuisine.

So while this book is arranged much as many a traditional cookbook – with sections on Breakfast, Light Meals, Mains, Desserts and Drinks, with an additional section on Feasting and Sharing – there is constant reference to the kindreds of Elves and their characteristics, so in association with the seafaring Teleri, for example, you will find plenty of fish and seafood dishes while for the woodland-loving Sindarin, you'll find an array of delicious recipes focused on game, nuts and berries.

Kindred by kindred, landscape by landscape, the book aims to build up an imaginary picture of the cuisine of the Elves. Forget The Prancing Pony or the taverns of Minas Tirith – the best food to be had in Middle-earth is in the halls of the Elves. Eat, drink and be merry!

Genealogy of the Races of Elves

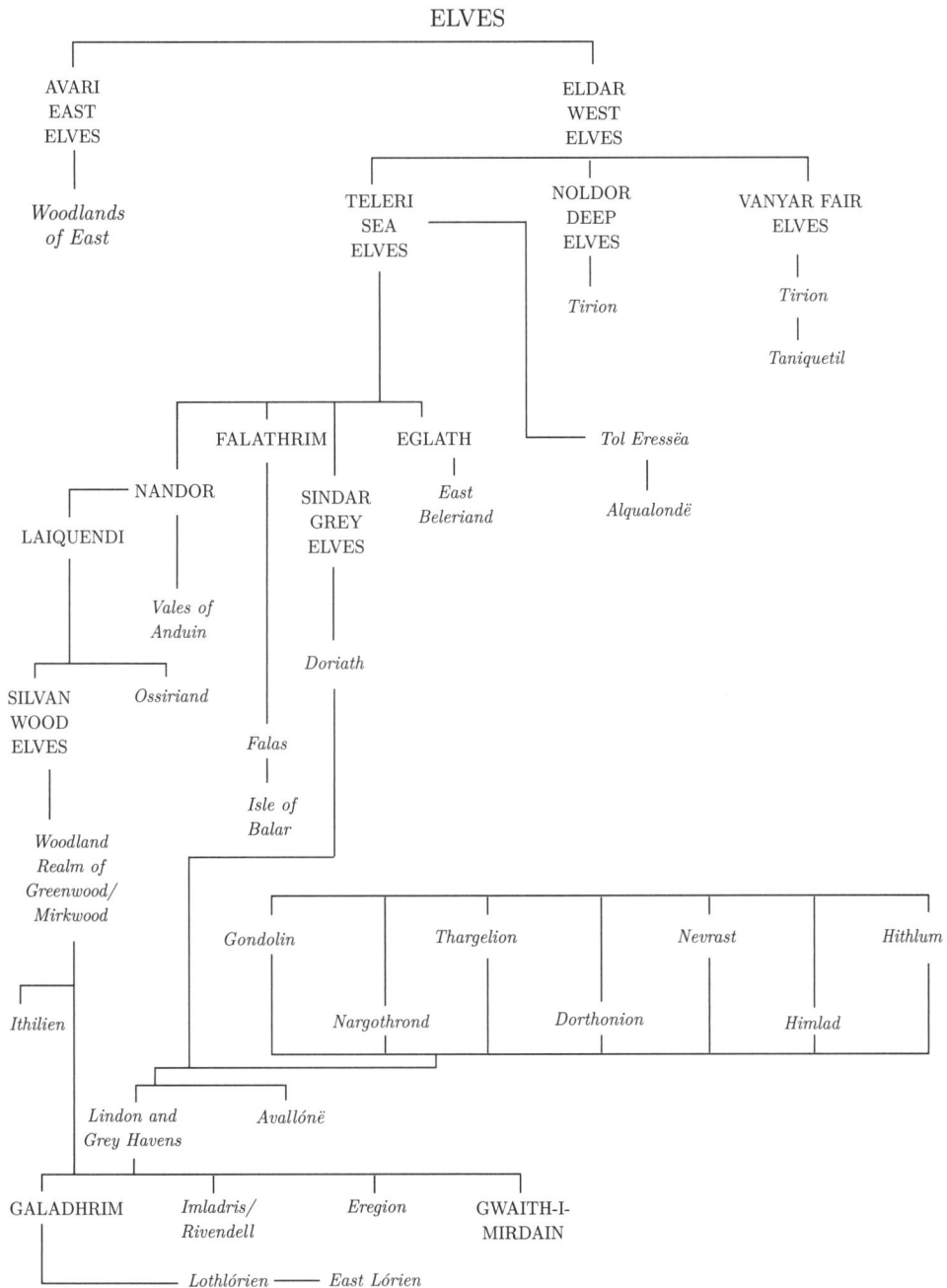

ELVES

AVARI
EAST
ELVES

ELDAR
WEST
ELVES

TELERI
SEA
ELVES

NOLDOR
DEEP
ELVES

VANYAR FAIR
ELVES

*Woodlands
of East*

Tirion

Tirion

Taniquetil

FALATHRIM

EGLATH

Tol Eressëa

NANDOR

SINDAR
GREY
ELVES

*East
Beleriand*

Alqualondë

LAIQUENDI

*Vales of
Anduin*

SILVAN
WOOD
ELVES

Ossiriand

Doriath

Falas

*Isle of
Balar*

*Woodland
Realm of
Greenwood/
Mirkwood*

Gondolin

Thargelion

Nevrast

Hithlum

Ithilien

Nargothrond

Dorthonion

Himlad

*Lindon and
Grey Havens*

Avallónë

GALADHRIM

*Imladris/
Rivendell*

Eregion

GWAITH-I-
MIRDAIN

Lothlórien ——— *East Lórien*

Breakfast

Whether or not breakfast is the most important meal of the day nutritionally, it can undoubtedly be one of the most significant emotionally. After breakfast often comes leave-taking and the beginning of a journey (even if it's just the commute to the office) – a cherished home and loved ones must, temporarily, be left behind.

It is a scenario that recurs frequently in *The Lord of the Rings* – the sweet sorrow of parting and the subsequent yearning for home are among its most enduring themes – and no doubt Tolkien's own leave-taking from his new wife, Edith, and departure for the Western Front in 1916, at the height of World War I, played a role here, too. The novel is punctuated by such heart-wrenching moments – Frodo's reluctant departure from The Shire; the Hobbits' leave-taking from the House of Tom Bombadil; the heavy-hearted departure of the Company of the Ring from Rivendell and its subsequent, yet still heavier-hearted departure from the Elvish realm of Lothlórien – but, even so, breakfast is never quite forgotten. A long or difficult journey needs a well-filled stomach, after all.

So imagine yourself under the eaves of the Golden Wood, a long trip along the Great River is ahead of you – what would you choose for your breakfast as you bid farewell to the Elves and the beauty and safety of their realm?

Neldoreth Mushrooms

Woods and forests played an important role in Tolkien's imagination. The beech woods of Neldoreth in the Beleriand – the vast homelands of the Elves in the First Age – provide a prototype for the enchanted woods we find in both *The Hobbit* (northern Mirkwood) and *The Lord of the Rings* (Lothlórien).

The primary association of Neldoreth, however, is with Lúthien, the most beautiful of the Elves and a poetic incarnation of Tolkien's wife, Edith, with whom the author enjoyed many woodland walks. The love story of the Elf-maiden Lúthien and the mortal Beren haunted Tolkien through his life – a story that can be said to begin in Neldoreth where Beren first sees Lúthien dancing among the beech trees by moonlight.

Beechwoods in autumn are the perfect place for mushroom hunting, as any forager knows, and this simple dish will provide the perfect breakfast – whether we are in love or not.

Farl is traditional Irish potato bread and perfect for soaking up all the delicious garlicky mushroom cooking juices in this recipe. You could use thickly cut toasted wholemeal bread instead.

Serves 2
Prep + cook time 30 minutes

1 tablespoon olive oil

25 g (1 oz) unsalted butter

2 shallots, finely chopped

250 g (8 oz) mixed mushrooms, such as chestnut, portobello and button, trimmed and sliced

2 garlic cloves, chopped

1 tablespoon lemon juice

2 tablespoons chopped flat-leaf parsley

2 large eggs

4 ready-made potato farls, toasted

salt and pepper

1 tablespoon chopped chives, to garnish

1. Heat the oil with the butter in a frying pan over a high heat. Reduce the heat slightly, add the shallots and mushrooms and fry for 6 minutes, stirring occasionally, until the mushrooms are golden. Stir in the garlic and cook, stirring, for 1 minute.

2. Add the lemon juice to the mushroom mixture and season with salt and pepper.

3. Remove the pan from the heat and stir in the parsley. Keep warm while you poach the eggs.

4. Half-fill a separate frying pan with water and bring to a simmer. Break in the eggs and cook for 3 minutes. Place 2 potato farls on each serving plate and top with the mushroom mixture, then the eggs. Sprinkle with the chives and serve immediately.

Tirion Tomatoes

Tolkien famously banished tomatoes from Middle-earth. In the first edition of *The Hobbit* (1927), during the 'unexpected party' with which the tale begins, Gandalf orders the poor, beleaguered Hobbit Bilbo Baggins to fetch cold chicken and tomatoes from his larder. By the third edition (1966), however, the 'tomatoes' had been replaced with 'pickles', since the fruit by now was considered an anachronism in Tolkien's conception of Middle-earth, which represents the Old World in a phase of its history many thousands of years before our own.

Side-stepping this thorny issue, we might indulgently imagine that Gandalf, in the original version, is recalling his former life as Olórin in Aman, the Blessed Realm – an American-like continent lying to the far west of Middle-earth, where both olvar (plants) and kelvar (animals) are different from those across the Great Sea. No doubt, tomatoes – the tomatl ('swelling fruit') of the Aztecs – were among the olvar of Aman and were a popular dish among the Eldar (the High Elves) living there. Accordingly, we've named these delicious stuffed tomatoes for Tirion, the crystal-white city of Eldamar, the 'Elven-home' in Aman.

⌐——···——⌐

Stuffed with fresh herbs and soft cheese, these tomatoes are a great choice for brunch, served with buttered toast – try Yavanna's Wholewheat & Sunflower Bread on page 29. They're very forgiving so won't mind being left to cook in the oven for longer if you forget about them.

Serves 4
Prep + cook time 30 minutes

250 g (8 oz) ricotta or cream cheese
2 spring onions, finely chopped
4 tablespoons chopped mixed herbs,
    such as chervil, chives, parsley, basil,
    marjoram and tarragon
finely grated rind of 1 lemon
1 tablespoon lemon juice
4 large beef tomatoes
salt and pepper

1. For the herby ricotta filling, mix together the ricotta or cream cheese with the spring onions, mixed herbs and lemon rind and juice. Season with salt and pepper and set aside.

2. Cut the tops off the tomatoes and scoop out the seeds. Stuff the tomatoes with the ricotta filling and transfer the tomatoes to a baking sheet. Bake in a preheated oven, 190°C (375°F) Gas Mark 5, for 20–25 minutes or until the tomatoes are tender.

Potato Rösti

There is something quintessentially Hobbitish about potatoes, of course. It's not just that Sam hankers after them in *The Lord of the Rings* and digs up 'tatties' to make his famous rabbit stew out in the wilderness, but that their earthy wholesomeness seems to sum up everything The Shire is about. Think of potatoes in Tolkien, and we may well imagine Master Samwise or his old dad, the Gaffer, digging over the kitchen garden at Bag End, ready to plant the next seed crop. Potatoes, for Hobbits, clearly mean hearth, home and happiness.

That doesn't mean to say, however, that the Elves are just too ethereal to eat the humble spud. They did not always live in fair cities or enchanted woodlands, after all. In *The Silmarillion*, Tolkien tells of the first awakening of the Elves in the far east of Middle-earth and the long journey westward of many of them in answer to the summons of the Valar. During that long trek, they endure many hardships, and they certainly wouldn't have turned their noses up at digging up a few tasty tubers to roast over their camp fires. They could only have dreamed of the potato rösti here, though.

The Elven Cookbook

Originating in Switzerland as a simple two-ingredient peasant dish, a rösti is essentially a giant hash brown or potato fritter. Golden and crispy, it is great served with bacon, as here, or topped with a poached egg or smoked salmon and soured cream.

Serves 4
Prep + cook time 40 minutes, plus cooling

3 potatoes, scrubbed but unpeeled, about 625 g (1¼ lb) total weight
½ onion, very thinly sliced
4 tablespoons vegetable oil
8 slices bacon
salt and pepper

To serve
1 large bunch of watercress
1 avocado, peeled, stoned and sliced (optional)

1. Cook the potatoes whole in a large saucepan of lightly salted boiling water for 8–10 minutes. Drain and set aside to cool. Once cooled, coarsely grate the potatoes and mix in a bowl with the sliced onion, 2 tablespoons of the oil and plenty of salt and pepper.

2. Heat the remaining oil in a large non-stick frying pan and add the rösti mixture, pushing down to flatten it so that it covers the base of the pan. Cook for 7–8 minutes, then slide on to an oiled plate or board. Flip the rösti back into the pan to cook the other side for 7–8 minutes until crisp and golden.

3. Meanwhile, fry the bacon and set aside to drain on some kitchen paper.

4. Cut the rösti into wedges, then arrange on serving plates, scatter over the watercress and top with the bacon. Add some slices of avocado, if using, and serve immediately.

Beren's Vegan Scramble

We might call Beren, a scion of the House of Bëor, a kind of honorary Elf. He falls in love with the Elvish princess Lúthien, he is the forefather of the Peredhil – the Half-elves – including Elrond and Arwen, and his story is closely entwined with the tragic history of Beleriand and the Elvish struggle over the Silmarils (page 25). In his youth, he even lives like we might hope Elves would (though in reality they fall far short) – wandering free in the wilderness of Dorthonion, becoming close to the birds and animals, and refraining from eating meat. Since he is unlikely to have eaten cheese or eggs during this time (though there might have been wild honey to be had), he is as close as to being a vegan as we can find in Tolkien's world.

This meat-less breakfast dish, then, is for the greatest hero of the Edain in the First Age.

For a healthy and satisfying vegan take on scrambled eggs, try this protein-packed tofu and mushroom scramble. The mushroom ketchup adds a deep umami flavour to the dish. Serve it with hash browns or hot toast.

Serves 4
Prep + cook time 15 minutes

2 tablespoons rapeseed or olive oil
200 g (7 oz) chestnut mushrooms, trimmed and quartered
250 g (8 oz) firm tofu, drained, patted dry and crumbled
125 g (4 oz) baby plum tomatoes, halved
1 tablespoon mushroom ketchup
3 tablespoons chopped flat-leaf parsley
salt and pepper

1. Heat the oil in a frying pan, add the mushrooms and cook over a high heat, stirring frequently, for 2 minutes until browned and softened. Add the tofu and cook, stirring, for 1 minute.

2. Add the tomatoes to the pan and cook for 2 minutes until starting to soften. Stir in the mushroom ketchup and half the parsley and season with salt and pepper.

3. Serve immediately, sprinkled with the remaining parsley.

Bilbo's Rivendell Breakfast

We all know that Hobbits like their food, and that, of course, begins with breakfast. Bilbo Baggins and his compatriots would certainly concur with the old idea that we should 'breakfast like a king'. We might wonder and worry, then, how Bilbo fares when he goes into retirement in Rivendell, the hidden Elvish town in the foothills of the Misty Mountains, at the beginning of *The Lord of the Rings*. During his residence of almost two decades there he spends his days researching and recording Elvish lore and history (as well as writing down his own adventures), so he would have needed an especially hearty breakfast to prepare him for his day in Rivendell's ancient library.

Perhaps we needn't fret. Rivendell's ruler, Elrond, clearly has a soft spot for the ageing Hobbit and perhaps made sure that the Elvish cooks rustled up a good breakfast for him, like this one, with a good creamy cheese made from the milk of the secret valley's wild mountain goats.

⸻ ··· ⸻

This is a great recipe for a leisurely Sunday breakfast. The addition of mustard adds a piquant note to the omelette which is filled with oozy melting goats' cheese. Add some basil-speckled fried tomatoes for a more colourful plate.

Serves 4
Prep + cook time 30 minutes

4 tablespoons olive oil
500 g (1 lb) mixed red and yellow
   cherry tomatoes, halved
a little basil, chopped, plus a few
   sprigs, to garnish
12 eggs
2 tablespoons wholegrain mustard
50 g (2 oz) butter
100 g (3½ oz) soft goats' cheese,
   diced
salt and pepper
watercress, to garnish

1. Heat the oil in a frying pan, add the tomatoes and cook over a medium heat for 2–3 minutes until softened (you may have to do this in 2 batches). Add the basil and season to taste with salt and pepper, then transfer to a bowl and keep warm.

2. Beat the eggs with the mustard in a large bowl and season with salt and pepper.

3. Melt one-quarter of the butter in an omelette pan or small frying pan over a medium heat until it stops foaming, then swirl in one-quarter of the egg mixture. Fork over the omelette so that it cooks evenly. As soon as it is set on the bottom (but still a little runny in the middle), dot over a quarter of the goats' cheese and cook for a further 30 seconds. Carefully slide the omelette onto a plate, folding it in half as you do so. Keep warm.

4. Repeat with the remaining mixture to make 3 more omelettes. Serve with the tomatoes, garnished with watercress and basil sprigs.

Sirion Cured Salmon

Great rivers – the Nile, the Ganges, the Euphrates, the Mississippi – have always played an important role in human history as cradles of civilization and highways linking disparate territories and peoples. It's no surprise, then, to discover similar great rivers in Middle-earth. In *The Hobbit* and *The Lord of the Rings* it is the Anduin – the Great River of Wilderland – and in Beleriand, the lands of the Elves in *The Silmarillion*, it is the Sirion, another north–south flowing river that provides the unifying feature in a diverse landscape.

The Sirion makes repeated appearances in Tolkien's tales of Beleriand. Perhaps its closest association there is with the golden-haired Elven king Finrod – the older brother of Galadriel – who builds a guard tower, Minas Tirith, on Tol Sirion, the 'island of Sirion', at the river's upper reaches. Finrod and his companions often wander along the banks of the Sirion, and though this recipe is an easy at-home cured version, we might well imagine them smoking their own freshly caught salmon from this wild, untamed river over their open campfires.

Served with scrambled eggs for a luxurious breakfast, cured salmon is delicious and a lot easier to make than you'd think. The basic recipe is equal parts salt and sugar plus flavourings – here coriander seeds and orange.

Serves 10 as a starter
Prep time 20 minutes, plus
  curing

600 g (1 lb 2 oz) salmon joint
175 g (6 oz) fine sea salt
175 g (6 oz) light brown soft sugar
1 teaspoon black peppercorns
2 teaspoons coriander seeds
Finely grated rind of 3 oranges

1. The day before you want to serve this, rinse the salmon fillet with cold water and pat it dry with kitchen paper.

2. Blitz the salt, sugar, peppercorns, coriander seeds and orange rind in a food processor, then scatter roughly a third of the cure mix across the bottom of a shallow dish or plastic container big enough to hold the fish. Sit the salmon skin side down on the mixture, then top with the remaining cure, rubbing it all over. Cover the salmon with clingfilm and leave in the fridge for 8–12 hours.

3. Remove from the fridge and rinse thoroughly with cold water and pat dry with kitchen paper. If you get a chance, the fish will benefit from a couple of hours of extra drying time, left uncovered on a plate in the fridge. Slice thinly, starting from the widest end of the fillet and serve.

Círdan's Golden Kedgeree

Not just for breakfast – you can tuck into this soothing fish, egg and rice dish, with its mildly spicy curry flavour, any time of day. It makes a great winter brunch or supper dish.

Serves 4
Prep + cook time 40 minutes

200 ml (7 fl oz) milk

150 ml (¼ pint) cold water

1 bay leaf

400 g (13 oz) undyed smoked haddock

3 tablespoons boiling water

pinch of saffron threads

1 tablespoon vegetable oil

25 g (1 oz) butter

1 onion, finely chopped

1 garlic clove, finely chopped

1 teaspoon peeled and finely grated fresh root ginger

1 teaspoon mild curry powder

250 g (8 oz) basmati rice

400 ml (1¼ pints) fish or vegetable stock

6 quails' eggs

5 tablespoons crème fraîche

salt and pepper

chopped flat-leaf parsley, to garnish

1. Put the milk, measured cold water and bay leaf in a shallow pan with a lid. Lay the haddock in the mixture, skin side down. Bring to the boil, cover and simmer for 5 minutes or until cooked through. Remove the haddock from the pan, reserving the milk mixture, and allow to cool.

2. Pour the measured boiling water over the saffron in a jug and leave to infuse.

3. Meanwhile, heat the oil and butter in a large saucepan. Add the onion and gently cook for 5 minutes until softened. Stir in the garlic and ginger and cook for a further 1 minute. Add the curry powder followed by the rice and stir until well coated.

4. Stir in the reserved milk mixture, stock and saffron with its soaking liquid. Bring to the boil, then leave to simmer for 15 minutes.

5. Meanwhile, bring a saucepan of water to the boil. Carefully lower in the quails' eggs and cook for 3 minutes. Remove from the pan and cool under cold running water, then shell and halve.

6. Remove the skin from the cooled fish, flake into chunks and add to the rice with the egg halves. Take off the heat, cover and leave to stand for 5 minutes to warm through. Gently stir in the crème fraîche and season. Spoon on to plates and scatter with chopped parsley to serve.

The Sindarin Elf Círdan is one of the most enduring but also most elusive figures in Tolkien's legendarium, playing a part in all four ages in the history of Middle-earth. He makes his last appearance at the close of *The Lord of the Rings*, where he welcomes the Ring-bearers Frodo, Bilbo, Galadriel and Gandalf, to his realm of the Grey Havens (Mithlond), before they set off on their voyage into the West.

Throughout, Círdan's closest associations are with the sea and shipbuilding – his very name means 'Shipwright' – and his people are known as the Falathrim – the 'people of the shore'. In myth, shipbuilders are often portrayed as being beacons of hope and having the gift of foresight – we have only to think of the biblical Noah and his ark – and Círdan persistently plays this role, even if he remains a largely shadowy figure.

This breakfast dish commemorates not only the Shipwright's love of the sea but his role as the keeper of one of the three Elven rings, Narya, the Ring of Fire (page 79), before he later passes it on to Gandalf. Narya's flame colour is mirrored in the gorgeous, golden saffron used here.

114

Woodhall Apple Cake

One of the most enchanting moments in *The Lord of the Rings* is the Hobbits' early encounter with a wandering company of High Elves, led by Gildor Inglorion, at Woody End, a wild, wooded area close to the eastern border of the Shire. Part of the magic of this brief scene is that we seem to see it largely through the eyes of Sam, for whom it is his first meeting with the Fair Folk. The wonder of this happy meeting and the impromptu meal the Hobbits enjoy at Woodhall remains etched in his memory ever after.

He is above all enraptured by the Elves' singing but he also recalls the sweetness of the fruits they serve. He ever after wishes he could grow apples like those he tasted that night. The apple (Sindarin: cordof) seems to have a close association with the Elves, who in turn associate it in their tales and songs with the long-lost Entwives – the spirit-guardians of orchards and plants (page 144).

This super-easy and beautifully moist apple cake is perfect for breakfast or afternoon tea. You can ring the changes by replacing the lemon rind and juice with orange rind and juice or replacing half the lemon rind and juice with lime.

Serves 10
Prep + cook time 1½ hours, plus cooling

100 g (3½ oz) dried apples, roughly chopped
100 ml (3½ fl oz) water
175 g (6 oz) slightly salted butter, softened
finely grated rind of 2 lemons
3 tablespoons lemon juice
175 g (6 oz) caster sugar
3 eggs
250 g (8 oz) self-raising flour
50 g (2 oz) poppy seeds

For the icing
75 g (3 oz) icing sugar, sifted
1 tablespoon lemon juice

1. Put the apples and measured water in a small saucepan and heat for 5 minutes until the apples have absorbed the water. Leave to cool.

2. Beat together the remaining cake ingredients in a bowl until pale and creamy. Stir in the cooled apples.

3. Spoon the mixture into a greased and lined 1 kg (2 lb) or 1.3 litre (2¼ pint) loaf tin and level the surface. Bake in a preheated oven, 160°C (325°F), Gas Mark 3, for 1–1¼ hours or until firm to the touch and a skewer inserted into the centre comes out clean. Loosen the cake at the ends and transfer to a wire rack. Peel off the lining paper and leave to cool.

4. Make the icing. Beat together the icing sugar and lemon juice in a bowl to make a smooth, spoonable icing. If necessary, add a few drops of water or extra lemon juice. Spoon over the cake so that it runs down the sides.

Aman Cornbread Muffins

In Middle-earth, wheat seems to be the main cereal crop – both the Hobbits' homeland, The Shire, and the South-kingdom of the Dúnedain, Gondor (and no doubt other settled places inhabited by Men), seem to have plentiful wheatfields and there is an abundance of reference to foods made from wheat, such as bread, biscuits and cakes. The Elves of Middle-earth grow wheat, too, though perhaps on a much smaller scale.

Wheat is also grown in Aman, the continent across the Sundering Sea. The New World crop now known in Europe as maize and in America as corn remains unmentioned, but we can well imagine it growing in abundance in the Undying Lands. In Pre-Columbian times, the cultivation of maize spread from southern Mexico across much of the Americas, and in Tolkien's world we might think of it being grown by the Vanyar, the fairest and noblest of the Elves who from even before the First Age dwelt exclusively in Aman. Their blond hair is certainly suggestive of golden corn fields and the brilliant, sunshine-colour of the maize ears, the corn cobs.

⌐——··——⌐

Whip up a batch of these cornbread muffins for a weekend breakfast treat to serve alongside crispy bacon or scrambled or poached eggs. They're best eaten warm but also freeze well and are great for lunchboxes and picnics.

Makes 12
Prep + cook time 40 minutes

75 g (3 oz) butter
1 large sweetcorn cob, kernels sliced off
1 small onion, diced
½ red chilli, deseeded and diced
140 g (4¾ oz) plain flour
140 g (4¾ oz) polenta
2 teaspoons baking powder
50g (2 oz) grated Cheddar cheese
pinch of salt
2 eggs
300 ml (½ pint) buttermilk
100 ml (3½ fl oz) milk

1. Melt 25g (1 oz) butter in a saucepan over a medium heat, add the sweetcorn, onion and chilli and cook for 2–3 minutes.

2. Sift together the flour, polenta and baking powder. Stir in the grated Cheddar and a pinch of salt.

3. Melt the remaining butter in a small saucepan. In a bowl, whisk together the eggs, melted butter, buttermilk and milk. Stir the wet ingredients into the dry, add the sweetcorn mixture and mix lightly. Divide between the holes of a greased 12-hole muffin tin.

4. Bake in a preheated oven, 190°C (375°F), Gas Mark 5, for 18–20 minutes until golden and cooked through.

Silmaril Breakfast Friands

The *Silmarillion* – Tolkien's account of the First Age – takes its name from the Silmarils – three jewels created by the proud Noldor Elf Fëanor, filled with the light of the Two Trees of Valinor. Of extraordinary beauty, the Silmarils provide a leitmotif for the tales, as they are coveted and fought over by Elves, Men, Dwarves and the Dark Lord Morgoth – in an epic struggle that culminates in the War of the Jewels and the catastrophic destruction of Beleriand. The jewels – both miraculous and seemingly cursed – play a similar role to the Necklace of Harmonia in the downfall of Thebes in Greek mythology or the Brísingamen necklace in Norse legends and tales.

These delicate breakfast friands, studded with jewel-like fruit, may not be quite as transcendently beautiful as the legendary Silmarils, but they may well have the power to create dissension around the breakfast table over who will get the last one!

continued overleaf ⇉

Made with egg whites and very little flour, these fruit-spiked friands are beautifully light while the ground almonds ensure they are moist and just the right kind of chewy. Delicious with a cup of coffee for an indulgent breakfast.

Makes 12
Prep + cook time 40 minutes, plus cooling

175 g (6 oz) unsalted butter

75 g (3 oz) dried strawberries, sour cherries or cranberries, roughly chopped

2 tablespoons orange juice

6 egg whites

225 g (7½ oz) caster sugar, plus extra for sprinkling

75 g (3 oz) plain flour

125 g (4 oz) ground almonds

1. Melt the butter and leave to cool. Put the strawberries, cherries or cranberries and orange juice in a saucepan and heat until the mixture is hot, then turn into a bowl and leave to cool.

2. Whisk the egg whites in a large clean bowl with a hand-held electric whisk until frothy and increased in volume but not peaking. Add the sugar, flour and ground almonds and stir in until almost combined. Drizzle the melted butter over the mixture, then stir together gently until just combined.

3. Divide the mixture evenly between the holes of a greased 12-hole muffin tray, then scatter the strawberries, cherries or cranberries on top. Bake in a preheated oven, 200°C (400°F), Gas Mark 6, for about 20 minutes until pale golden and just firm to the touch. Leave in the tin for 5 minutes, then transfer to a wire rack to cool. Serve sprinkled with caster sugar.

Teiglin Roast Hazelnut Muesli

In his creation of Middle-earth, Tolkien developed an especially rich and elaborate flora, encompassing both real-world species (or relatives thereof) and imaginary ones. Thus, alongside tree species such as oak and beech, we also find entirely fictional ones such as the kingly Mallorn, which flourishes in Lothlórien. Whatever their origin – in nature or fancy – Tolkien describes them in loving detail, so that as we walk about the Shire with the Hobbits or wander about Beleriand with the heroes of *The Silmarillion*, we develop a deep appreciation for Middle-earth's landscapes and the living things that dwell in them.

One especially common real-world species we comes across in Middle-earth is the hazel, or filbert. In Beleriand, it is depicted growing in stands about the wooded banks of the River Teiglin – a tributary of the Sirion (page 19) and its nuts, which become especially sweet when roasted, were no doubt eaten by both Elves and Men alike.

Full of good things and no nasties, homemade muesli makes sure you start your day the right way. You can vary the dried fruit: try dried cranberries or apricots, chopped dates, goji berries or currants.

Serves 4
**Prep + cook time 25 minutes,
  plus cooling**

100 g (3½ oz) shredded dried coconut

100 g (3½ oz) flaked almonds

100 g (3½ oz) blanched hazelnuts

100 g (3½ oz) sunflower seeds

250 g (8 oz) buckwheat flakes

250 g (8 oz) millet flakes

100 g (3½ oz) dried mango, sliced

100 g (3½ oz) sultanas

1. Spread the coconut out in a thin layer on a baking sheet. Spread the flaked almonds, hazelnuts and sunflower seeds out in a thin layer on a second baking sheet. Toast in a preheated oven, 150°C (300°F), Gas Mark 2, for about 20 minutes, stirring every 5 minutes to make sure it browns evenly. Keep a close eye on the sunflower seeds and don't let them burn.

2. Remove the trays from the oven and leave to cool, then roughly chop the hazelnuts.

3. Mix the toasted mixture will all the remaining ingredients in a large bowl until well combined. Store in an airtight container for up to 1–2 weeks.

Yavanna's Wholewheat Bread

In *The Silmarillion*, wheat is described growing tall and golden in the fields of Yavanna in Valinor, the realm of the Valar – the great spirits who helped form Arda (the Earth) after its creation. For Tolkien, Valinor – a part of the continent of Aman – was clearly closely akin to the lands of plenty that abound in the world's mythologies – from the Vanaheimr of the Norse myths, home to the Vana, gods of fertility, to the Cockaigne of medieval legend. It is tempting to draw comparisons, too, with the legends that quickly grew up around the Americas after the first arrival of Europeans in the late fifteenth century – as a continent blessed with oversized fruits and vegetables and a superabundance of game.

The nurturing figure of Yavanna herself is heavily indebted to mythological goddesses such as the Greek Demeter, the Roman Ceres and the Norse Sif, all closely associated with the grain harvest, though Yavanna's remit as Tolkien's 'Mother Earth' runs to all living creatures and plants. Nurture yourself by making this wholesome loaf made from the 'ancient grain' known as spelt and imagine yourself breakfasting looking out over the blissful, sunny landscapes of Valinor.

Is there anything better than the aroma of freshly baked bread? Needing no proving time and no kneading, this sunflower-studded loaf is super-quick to rustle up for a weekend breakfast. Serve warm with butter and a dollop of Bramble & Fig Jam (see page 32).

Makes 1 loaf
Prep + cook time 1 hour

200 g (7 oz) plain flour, plus extra for dusting
200 g (7 oz) wholemeal spelt flour
100 g (3½ oz) rye flour
2 teaspoons baking powder
1 teaspoon salt
75 g (3 oz) sunflower seeds, plus 2 tablespoons
500 g (1 lb) natural yogurt
milk, to glaze

1. Mix together the flours, baking powder, salt and the 75 g (3 oz) sunflower seeds in a bowl. Stir in the yogurt and mix to a fairly soft dough.

2. Shape the dough into a log on a floured surface, then drop into a greased 1.25 kg (2½ lb) or 1.5 litre (2½ pint) loaf tin. Brush with a little milk and sprinkle with the remaining sunflower seeds.

3. Bake in a preheated oven, 220°C (425°F), Gas Mark 7, for 20 minutes. Reduce the oven temperature to 160°C (325°F), Gas Mark 3, and bake for a further 30 minutes. The base of the bread should sound hollow when tapped. If necessary, return to the oven for a little longer. Transfer to a wire rack to cool.

Gondolin Rose-Petal Jelly

Hidden mountain kingdoms are a common motif in myth and legend – from the utopian Shambhala of East Asian Buddhism to the fabled city of gold El Dorado, long searched for by the Spanish conquistadors. In Tolkien, the quintessential hidden kingdom is Gondolin, founded just after the beginning of the First Age by the Noldorin lord Turgon. Hidden within the Encircling Mountains, in the north of Beleriand, it can be reached only by a closely guarded Hidden Way.

In his voluminous notes, Tolkien imagined Gondolin in some detail – its gates, streets, squares and buildings. It was renowned for its marble houses and its flower gardens, and especially, it seems, for its fragrant roses. The Alley of Roses, close to the king's palace, is noted as an especially beautiful place to walk in. The city was destroyed by the forces of Morgoth in FA 510, a catastrophe recounted as one of the so-called 'Great Tales' told in *The Silmarillion* and in *The Fall of Gondolin*. Recapture something of the lost beauty of this hidden Noldorin kingdom in this fragrant rose-petal jelly.

***

Delicate and lightly fragrant, this softly set jelly is lovely on hot crumpets, swirled into thick yogurt or spooned over porridge. It's important to make it with rose petals that haven't been sprayed with any kind of chemical. The rose petals may lose their colour during the cooking process but don't panic – the lemon juice will restore the colour!

Makes 3 jars
Prep + cook time 50 minutes

350 ml (12 fl oz) water
70 g (2½ oz) unsprayed rose petals, washed
400 g (14 oz) granulated sugar
3 tablespoons lemon juice
1 teaspoon pectin

1. Place the measured water and rose petals in a saucepan over a low heat and simmer gently for 10 minutes. Add three-quarters of the sugar and stir to dissolve the sugar crystals. Add the lemon juice and simmer for a further 10 minutes.

2. Meanwhile, mix the remaining sugar and pectin in a small bowl. Add to the jelly a little at time, stirring constantly to make sure the pectin doesn't clump. Simmer for a further 20 minutes.

3. The jelly will still be quite runny – it will firm up as it sets and cools but the texture stays syrupy rather than thick.

4. Ladle into sterilized, warm, dry jars. Cover with screw-top lids and leave to cool. This will keep for up to 2 months in the fridge or can be frozen for up to 6 months.

Ithilien Bramble Jam

As any rambler knows, brambles – blackberries – can be both a pleasure and a nuisance. The fruit is a sweet juicy treat for the walker, but, gathering in great thorny thickets, can offer a prickly hinderance along the path. In Tolkien's Mordor, the blighted land of Sauron, there are even 'super-brambles', with knife-like thorns, that bear more than a passing resemblance to the concertinaed barbed-wire fences, experienced by Tolkien and many other soldiers during the First World War.

The Brambles of Mordor's rather gentler cousins are also shown growing in Ithilien, the once-fair land to the east of Gondor that has been blighted by the evildoings of Sauron and the Morgul-king. After the end of the War of the Rings, the Sindarin Elf Legolas settles with some of his people in Ithilien and works to restore its woodlands to their former glory. It would be nice to think that the bramble – usually a sign of neglect – would not be entirely banished and that – tamed and tended – would be used by the Elves to make a wonderful jam, much like this one.

The trickiest part of making jam is knowing when it has reached setting point. An easy way to tell is to drop a teaspoon of jam onto a saucer that's been chilled in the fridge or freezer. The jam will quickly cool to room temperature. Push the jam gently with your finger – the skin will wrinkle if it's ready. If it's not, return the jam to the heat and boil it again and re-test in a few minutes.

Makes 4 jars
Prep + cook time 50 minutes

500 g (1 lb) blackberries
500 g (1 lb) figs (about 9), quartered
300 ml (½ pint) water
2 cinnamon sticks, halved
1 kg (2 lb) granulated sugar, warmed
juice of 1 lemon
15 g (½ oz) butter (optional)

1. Add the blackberries and figs to a large saucepan. Pour in the measured water, then add the cinnamon sticks. Bring to a simmer, then simmer, uncovered, for about 10 minutes, until the fruit is just beginning to soften.

2. Pour the sugar into the pan and add the lemon juice. Heat gently, stirring from time to time, until the sugar has dissolved. Bring to the boil, then boil rapidly until setting point (see above) is reached – about 25 minutes. Skim with a draining spoon or stir in butter if needed (this will help to break up any foamy scum on the surface).

3. Ladle into sterilized, warm, dry jars, filling to the very top and discarding the cinnamon sticks. Cover with screw-top lids, or with waxed discs and cellophane tops secured with elastic bands. Label and leave to cool.

Arwen's Bilberry Jam

Bilberries seem to grow in thickets in the foothills of the Misty Mountains: in *The Lord of the Rings*, Aragorn and the four Hobbits seek refuge from the Black Riders in the deep heather and bilberry brushwood as they hazard the final stretch to Rivendell along the Great East–West Road. We may well imagine, then, that bilberries are one of the popular gathered fruits of the Rivendell Elves, made into jams and compotes or as an accompaniment to roasted meats.

This delicious bilberry jam might be a particular favourite of Aragorn, a treat made and served by the Half-Elven Arwen Undómiel to her betrothed on one of his rare visits to her father's realm. Even weather-beaten heroes like a few simple pleasures in their lives.

This easy-to-make berry jam uses frozen blueberries for convenience and is perfect with hot scones or toast. For a grown-up spin, you can stir a teaspoon of whisky or gin into each jar of jam before covering and storing.

Makes 4–5 jars
Prep + cook time 30 minutes

2 x 480 g (15¼ oz) packs frozen
   blueberries
340 g (12 oz) fresh raspberries
1 kg (2 lb) jam sugar with pectin
15 g (½ oz) butter (optional)

1. Add the frozen blueberries and the raspberries to a large saucepan. Cover and cook gently for 10 minutes, stirring from time to time, until the juices run and the fruit begins to soften.

2. Pour the sugar into the pan and heat gently, stirring from time to time, until dissolved. Bring to the boil, then boil rapidly until setting point is reached (see page 32) – about 5–10 minutes. Skim with a draining spoon or stir in butter if needed (this will help to break up any foamy scum on the surface).

3. Ladle into sterilized, warm, dry jars, filling to the very top. Cover with screw-top lids, or with waxed discs and cellophane tops secured with elastic bands. Label and leave to cool.

Edhellond Almond Butter

The haven of Edhellond was the most southerly settlement of the Sindarin Elves in Middle-earth, founded by refugees from war-torn Beleriand during the First Age. It is the setting of the tragic finale of one of Tolkien's saddest love stories, the story of Amroth, king of Lothlórien, and the Elf-maid Nimrodel. By the time of the events narrated in *The Lord of the Rings*, the haven has long since been abandoned, though the mortal rulers of the surrounding lands, the Princes of Dol Amroth, are said to have Elvish blood, being descendants of a Númenórean lord and one of Nimrodel's companions, Mithrellas.

Edhellond, like the kingdom of Gondor of which in the Third Age it became a part, would have enjoyed a warm, sunny, Mediterranean-type climate, perfect for the cultivation of almond trees, with their glorious pinkish-white blossoms. It is perfectly possible, then, that the Elves of Edhellond made something akin to this delicious almond butter and that they later passed the secret of its making to the Gondorians, passed down the line of the Princes of Dol Amroth.

⌒—··—⌒

Homemade nut butter is healthy, cheap, uncomplicated to make and tastes so much better than anything you can buy. Add honey or maple syrup, a hint of vanilla extract and a pinch of cinnamon to make it extra-special, if you like.

Makes 300 g (10 oz)
Prep + cook time 20 minutes

300 g (10 oz) skin-on almonds
drizzle of honey or maple syrup
few drops of vanilla extract (optional)
ground cinnamon, to taste (optional)

1. Spread the almonds evenly on a baking tray and roast in a preheated oven, 190°C (170°F), Gas Mark 5, for about 10 minutes, making sure to turn them or give them a toss halfway through. Be careful not to let the nuts burn. Remove from the oven and leave to cool.

2. Put the almonds into a food processor and whizz for 10 minutes, stopping every now and then to scrape down the sides with a spatula if necessary. When the almonds are your desired consistency, add the honey or maple syrup, and vanilla extract and cinnamon, if using, and whizz for another 30 seconds until well combined.

3. Store in a sealed container in the fridge for up to 3 weeks.

Radagast's Homemade Oat Milk

We know that the Elves of the Great Greenwood (Mirkwood) were far from being vegetarian, but this oat milk may well have delighted them when, while passing south to visit their kindred in Lothlórien, they were treated to a glass of it at Rhosgobel, the home of the Wizard Radagast the Brown. In Valinor he was a Maia in the service of Yavanna, and on his mission to Middle-earth was especially concerned with its animals and plants. We know nothing of his dietary habits, but he is unlikely to have been a meat-eater as we know Gandalf to have been – so this oat milk might have been just the thing for him to make. The oats, of course, would have been traded through his Northmen neighbours, the Beornings.

Making your own oat milk allows you to control the ingredients and is very easy to do. You can customize it to suit your taste by adding a dash of vanilla extract, a couple of dates or a little maple syrup or honey to sweeten.

Makes about 750 ml (26 fl oz)
**Prep time 20 minutes, plus
  soaking and straining**

100 g (3½ oz) rolled oats
750 ml (26 fl oz) cold water
  pinch of fine salt

1. Put the oats into a bowl and add water to cover them. Cover and set aside somewhere cool for 4 hours or overnight.

2. Strain the oats, discarding the soaking water. Add the oats to a food processor, along with the measured cold water and the salt. Blend until completely smooth and there are no pieces of oat visible.

3. Line a sieve with clean muslin and place over a bowl or jug. Pour in the oat milk, then leave to strain for 1 hour or until most of the liquid has drained into the bowl or jug. Gather together the sides of the muslin and squeeze tightly to extract the last of the milk.

4. Pour the milk into a bottle and store in the fridge. This will keep for 2–3 days.

Elvish Cuisines

We can conjecture that there was not a single Elvish cuisine but many. The diasporic spread of Tolkien's Elves from the far east of Middle-earth – where they first appeared – to its western regions and shores, and from there across the sea to Aman, together with the vast ages that passed between their Awakening and the 'present' of *The Lord of the Rings*, would have ensured that a wealth of cooking styles and preferences evolved, at least as complex as the evolution of the Elvish kindreds (page 9). We can thus be pretty sure, for example, that the shore-dwelling and seafaring Teleri ate a fish-based diet, that the forest-dwelling Sindar consumed a lot of game and berries, and that the Noldor of, say, the city of Gondolin in Beleriand made good use of the produce of their farms, orchards and kitchen gardens.

Just as in human history, there would also have been a progression from relatively basic methods of cooking to more or less sophisticated ones. No doubt the 'primitive' Elves of Cuiviénen (the place where the Elves first awoke) all cooked in much the same way – over an open fire and using the simplest of gathered and hunted ingredients from sea and forest – but by the time of the First Age the Eldar at least must have developed more civilized cooking methods. They no doubt had ovens and a panoply of kitchen equipment at their disposal, and used produce they themselves had grown or reared, having been taught the arts of agriculture by the Valar, the Maiar and the Ent-wives. This development, however, would never have been clear cut or absolute. The Elves of Lothlórien or Rivendell – the 'latest' Elves we meet in the pages of Tolkien's books – no doubt never entirely gave up on their ancient hunter-gatherer ways and continued to cook, at least at times, over open fires, as indeed occurs in *The Hobbit* where there seems to be a contrast made between the food on offer down in the woods and that being served up in Elrond's halls.

For all this variety and difference, all this evolution, however, perhaps it is possible to speak of an Elvish cuisine in the singular – of characteristics that unite the way in which Elves cooked and ate across vast lengths of time and space, different from those of Men, Dwarves and Hobbits. We might, of course, pinpoint a preference for the fresh, the seasonal and the local – a diet that is as close to nature as can be – a diet, moreover, of moderation and lightness that works in harmony with the body and not against it, with the power to energize, not dissipate – but something more, too – the *je ne sais quoi* that elevates the extraordinary above the ordinary. Perhaps this is captured best early on in *The Lord of the Rings* when Frodo, Pippin and Sam eat an al fresco Elvish meal at Woody End, where, at least in the memory of the Hobbits, everything tastes at once dreamlike and yet more intense, more vivid, than anything they have tasted before.

Light Meals

Although several times in *The Hobbit* and *The Lord of the Rings* we catch the Elves dining on roasted meat or drinking heavy red wines, we are more likely to associate these ethereal beings with lighter fare than the heartier meals enjoyed, say, by Hobbits and Dwarves. To use French terminology, we would probably think of their culinary preferences as leaning more towards cuisine minceur ('lean cuisine') than cuisine bourgeoise. How else could Tolkien's Elves be so uniformly slender, fit and healthy?

The archetypal Elvish meal, then, may be that provided to the Hobbits by the Noldorin Elf Gildor in Woody End in The Shire in Chapter 3 of *The Lord of the Rings* – light, fresh, fragrant ... and memorable. Of the meal of bread, vegetables, fruits and drink brought by the Elves to the hall-like clearing, Pippin afterwards recalled that he felt as though he was in a 'waking dream'. Perhaps we cannot promise quite that effect with the recipes on offer in this section, but we hope to capture something of the Elvish spirit – food that leaves you feeling nourished but not overfull; food that uses simple ingredients, simply prepared, food that is, above all, memorable for you and your guests.

Greenwood Nettle Soup

Nettles grow abundantly in the woods and wild places of Middle-earth: Tolkien quite often mentions them, sometimes in association with other rampant, stinging, scratching or even toxic species such as thistle and hemlock. In the Old Forest, for example, such weed-like species are used symbolically, connoting a wilder, more dangerous world than the safety of the neighbouring Shire, with its cultivated fields of mushrooms, oats, tobacco and wheat.

We may well imagine, however, that the Elves, especially those known as the Laiquendi ('Green-elves'), who live in the woodlands of Middle-earth, knew how to make good use of nettles and of the rich source of vitamins and protein they contain – especially in the spring when the shoots are young and tender. Here, then, is a tasty soup that might have been made on a sunny spring day in the woodlands of Ossiriand or Greenwood the Great (Mirkwood).

This tasty dark-green soup makes the most of foraged nettles. For extra luxury, top with a swirl of thick cream before serving. Be sure to wear gloves when handling the nettles and wash them well in cold water before adding to the soup.

Serves 6
Prep + cook time 1 hour

25 g (1 oz) butter

1 onion, roughly chopped

1 baking potato, about 250 g (8 oz), diced

1 litre (1¾ pints) vegetable or chicken stock

¼ teaspoon grated nutmeg

225 g (7½ oz) nettle leaves, well washed and drained

300 ml (½ pint) milk

salt and pepper

1. Heat the butter in a saucepan, add the onion and fry gently for 5 minutes until softened. Add the potato, cover and cook for 10 minutes, stirring occasionally.

2. Pour in the stock, add the nutmeg and salt and pepper then bring to the boil. Cover and simmer for 20 minutes until the potato is soft. Add the nettle leaves to the pan. Re-cover the pan and cook for 5 minutes until just wilted.

3. Purée the soup in batches in a blender or food processor until smooth, then pour back into the saucepan, mix in the milk, gently reheat and serve.

The Elven Cookbook

Kine of Araw's Oxtail Soup

During the earliest ages of Arda (the Earth), Oromë, the Huntsman of the Valar, spends much of his time away from the splendours of Valinor, hunting the dark creatures of Melkor/Morgoth in the benighted continent of Middle-earth. Associated with him, in Elven lore, are the colossal, majestic cattle known as the Kine of Araw that roamed the eastern regions – Araw being the Vala's name in Sindarin.

The kine seem to be closely related to the sun (though the sun did not yet exist in earliest times). Tolkien describes their flanks as brilliant white, reflecting the sunlight at the Gates of Morning in the east – a detail that may relate to the cattle of the sun god Helios in Greek mythology. This deep-bodied soup might have been made by the Elves on winter days when they dreamed of their lost home in Valinor and the Valar and kindred who lived there.

Rich and comforting, this is the perfect meal when it's grey and cold outside. It improves with keeping, so any leftovers will be even better the following day. For a complete feast, serve with the Cornbread Muffins on page 24.

Serves 6
Prep + cook time 5 hours

1 tablespoon sunflower oil
500 g (1 lb) oxtail pieces, string
   removed
1 onion, finely chopped
2 carrots, diced
2 celery sticks, diced
200 g (7 oz) potatoes, diced
small bunch of mixed herbs
2 litres (3½ pints) beef stock
450 ml (¾ pint) strong ale
2 teaspoons English mustard
2 tablespoons Worcestershire sauce
1 tablespoon tomato purée
410 g (13½ oz) can butter beans,
   rinsed and drained
salt and pepper
chopped parsley, to garnish

1. Heat the oil in a large saucepan, add the oxtail pieces and fry until browned on one side. Turn the oxtail pieces over and add the onion, stirring until browned on all sides. Stir in the carrots, celery, potatoes and herbs and cook for 2–3 more minutes.

2. Pour in the stock and ale, then add the mustard, Worcestershire sauce, tomato purée and butter beans. Season well with salt and pepper and bring to the boil, stirring. Half cover the pan and simmer gently for 4 hours.

3. Lift the oxtail and herbs out of the pan with a slotted spoon. Discard the herbs and cut the meat off the oxtail bones, discarding any fat. Return the meat to the pan, reheat gently then taste and adjust the seasoning if needed. Ladle into bowls and sprinkle with the chopped parsley.

Alqualondëan Clam Soup

The principal city of Tol Eressëa (see page 45) is Alqualondë, which, despite its watery-sounding toponym, means 'Swanhaven' – named for the beautiful swan-shaped ships moored in its harbours. Its buildings, Tolkien tells us, are studded with pearls and the city is lit by many lamps.

Tolkien does not tell us what kind of pearl the Elves used to decorate their city, but perhaps they were clam, rather than oyster, pearls, and so may have been a by-product of Elvish clam fishing. Pearls from giant clams (genus Tridacna) can be exceptionally large – as in the famous Pearl of Lao Tzu, which is 24 centimetres (9½ inches) in diameter – and so would have provided good food as well as fine decoration.

Bursting with flavour and texture from the lardons, potatoes and clams, this hearty and creamy soup is a complete meal in a bowl. Be sure to discard any clams that are still closed after cooking.

Serves 4
Prep + cook time 45 minutes

15g (½ oz) butter
1 tablespoon vegetable oil
75g (3oz) lardons
1 onion, finely chopped
1 red chilli, finely chopped
100 ml (3½ fl oz) dry white wine
500ml (17 fl oz) milk
200ml (7 fl oz) double cream
200ml (7 fl oz) chicken stock
375g (12 oz) baby potatoes, halved
500g (1 lb) cleaned live clams
handful of chopped flat-leaf parsley,
   to garnish

1. Heat the butter and vegetable oil in a frying pan. Add the lardons and cook for about 5 minutes until golden brown. Remove from the pan. Add the onion and cook for about 7 minutes until softened.

2. Stir in the chilli and return the lardons to the pan. Pour in the wine and boil for about 2 minutes until reduced. Pour in the milk, double cream and chicken stock and bring to the boil.

3. Stir through the baby potatoes and cook for 10 minutes or until tender. Add the clams. Cover and cook for 5 minutes until the clams have opened, discarding any that remain closed.

4. Scatter over a handful of chopped flat-leaf parsley and serve.

Tol Eressëa Samphire Sea Salad

Tolkien was no stranger to plundering the world's mythologies to enrich his own, and one such flotsam of his plunder is Tol Eressëa – the floating island of Belegaer, the vast ocean between the two great continents of Middle-earth and Aman. In Homer's *The Odyssey* we find the floating island of Aeolia – the Isle of the Winds – and in Celtic legend Tír na nÓg – an elusive paradise floating somewhere off the Irish coast, appearing and disappearing in the Atlantic mists.

Tolkien's own floating island is used as an actual boat. Originally, the island was attached to the ocean floor, but after the Valar summon the Elves to Aman, the Vala of the sea, Ulmo, uproots the island and uses it as a giant vessel to transport the three kindreds across the ocean. Later, the island is once again anchored to the ocean floor, just off Aman, and becomes the home of the Teleri, the Sea-elves.

On their voyage across Belegaer, the Elves would surely have used the natural produce of their island-raft, foraging what they could from its shores. This fresh-tasting sea salad has as its principal ingredient samphire, which grows abundantly in salt marshes.

⌐ –··– ⌐

This salad is full of intense summer flavours and makes a lovely lunch on a hot day. Use really ripe tomatoes and be aware of samphire's inherent saltiness when seasoning – you won't need a lot of extra salt.

Serves 4
Prep time 15 minutes, plus standing

600 g (1¼ lb) large tomatoes, roughly chopped into 2 cm (¾ inch) pieces
1 teaspoon sea salt
200 g (7 oz) samphire, trimmed
150 g (5 oz) ciabatta bread
½ red onion, finely chopped
handful of basil leaves, plus extra to garnish
1 tablespoon red wine vinegar
2 tablespoons extra virgin olive oil
salt and pepper

1. Put the chopped tomatoes into a non-metallic bowl and sprinkle over the sea salt. Leave to stand for 1 hour.

2. Meanwhile, bring a saucepan of water to the boil, add the samphire and blanch for 1 minute. Drain the samphire and immediately place in a bowl of iced water. Drain and pat dry with kitchen paper.

3. Remove the crusts from the ciabatta and tear into rough chunks.

4. Give the tomatoes a good squash with clean hands, then add the samphire, ciabatta, onion, basil, vinegar and oil and season to taste with salt and pepper. Mix together carefully, then scatter over the remaining basil and serve.

Menegroth Endive & Pear Salad

It is not only Tolkien's Dwarves who build subterranean kingdoms, but his Elves, too. The most famous of these is the capital of the forest kingdom of Doriath, Menegroth – the city of a Thousand Caves, hewn deep into the side of a ravine. But there are other underground Elvish kingdoms and fortresses, too – Nargothrond, the stronghold of the Noldorin Elf lord Finrod, modelled on Menegroth; and, in *The Hobbit*, the subterranean halls of the Elvenking (Thranduil), who originally came from Doriath. In associating some of his Elves with such chthonic cities, Tolkien is probably alluding to the dark-elves – dökkálfar – of Norse mythology who, unlike the Ljósálfar (light-elves), live underground and seem to be (like some of Tolkien's Elves indeed) gifted smiths.

Dark and light come together in this flavoursome salad. Belgian endive, or witloof, is a sprouted chicory root grown indoors without sunlight and so might be thought uniquely suited to the Elves' cavernous kingdoms. Here it is teamed, however, with fragrant pears and rose petals – thus also associating it with the rose-garlanded Lúthien, bright daughter of Doriath's dark-browed king, Thingol.

This unconventional and very pretty Moroccan-inspired salad pairs crisp, mildly bitter endive with ripe pears steeped in rosewater. You don't have to use the rose petals but their aromatic, sweet flavour adds an extra dimension to this summery salad.

Serves 4
Prep time 10 minutes

2 ripe but firm pears, peeled, cored
 and thinly sliced
juice of ½ lemon
1–2 tablespoons rosewater
2 heads of white or Belgian endive,
 leaves separated and rinsed
1 tablespoon olive oil
1 teaspoon runny honey
small handful of fresh, scented rose
 petals
salt

1. Place the pears in a bowl and lightly toss with the lemon juice and rosewater. Leave to stand for 5 minutes.

2. Arrange the endive leaves in a shallow salad bowl. Remove the pear from the rosewater and lemon juice with a slotted spoon and scatter it over and around the chicory leaves.

3. Mix the oil with any rosewater and lemon juice left in the bowl and pour over the salad. Drizzle over the honey and sprinkle with salt. Scatter over the rose petals and toss just before serving.

Silverlode Smoked Trout

Tolkien spent the happiest years of his childhood in the hamlet of Sarehole (then in Worcestershire and now part of Birmingham) and fondly remembered playing on the banks of the small river that ran through it, the Cole. The Cole and Sarehole's busy watermill became the model for The Water and the Old Mill in The Shire, both seen prominently in his charming watercolour illustration The Hill: Hobbiton-across-the-Water, included in some editions of *The Hobbit*.

It is not surprising, then, that rivers, large and small, tributaries and streams, played such an important role in Tolkien's imagination and in his geography of Middle-earth, and are always given evocative names – the Withywindle, the Brandywine, Greyflood, Entwash …. The Silverlode (Celebrant in Sindarin) seems a more than appropriate name for the small river that runs from near the East-gate of the Dwarven mansions of Moria, through the Elven woodland-realm of Lothlórien, and finally into the Anduin, the Great River. It evokes at once the fast-flowing waters of the Silverlode itself, the diamond-hard, silver-coloured metal mithril mined in Moria, the white garments of Galadriel, Lothlórien's Elven-queen, possessor of the White Ring, Nenya … and perhaps, too, the silvery rainbow trout that might, we imagine, swim along its length.

Smoked trout has a more delicate flavour than the commonly used smoked salmon and pairs beautifully with the sweetness of the grapes in this salad. Serve it as an elegant starter or light lunch.

Serves 2
Prep time 15 minutes

200 g (7 oz) smoked trout
160 g (5½ oz) red seedless grapes
75 g (3 oz) watercress
1 fennel bulb

For the dressing
3 tablespoons mayonnaise
4 cornichons, finely diced
1½ tablespoons capers, chopped
2 tablespoons lemon juice
salt and pepper

1. Flake the smoked trout into bite-sized pieces, removing any bones, and place in a large salad bowl. Wash and drain the grapes and watercress and add them to the bowl. Finely slice the fennel and add to the mix.

2. Make the dressing by mixing the mayonnaise, cornichons, capers and lemon juice. Season to taste with salt and pepper, then carefully mix through the salad and serve.

Seaweed Cakes

Many of Tolkien's 'gods'– his Valar and Maiar – bear more than a passing resemblance to those of ancient real-world mythologies. Uinen, a Maia in the service of Ulmo, Lord of Waters, has a close affinity with such figures as the Greek sea-goddess Leucothea, who in Homer's *Odyssey* saves its shipwrecked hero, Odysseus, from drowning – quite apart from her associations with the mermaids of folklore (at least the kindly ones among them). Unlike her unruly husband, Ossë, who is forever whipping up storms, Uinen represents the more beneficent aspects of the sea – calm sunlit waters, the fruitful shore, and salt streams. The Teleri of the coasts of Beleriand had an especially close relationship with Uinen, as did the seafaring Men of Númenor, who prayed for her help out at sea.

Here we have imagined little sushi parcels that the Teleri prepared and ate in honour of Uinen, the wrappings made from the tangled masses of seaweed they gathered from the rock pools close to their havens and whose strands reminded them of the long hair of the Maia herself.

⌐—··—⌐

A picture on a plate, these little seaweed cakes are less fiddly to prepare than traditional rolled sushi but just as tasty. Serve with soy sauce and fiery wasabi for dipping and, if you like, some pickled ginger to accompany them.

Serves 4
Prep time 20 minutes

400 g (13 oz) cooked sushi rice
sushi rice seasoning, to taste
4 sheets of nori seaweed
100 g (3½ oz) smoked salmon
50 g (2 oz) cucumber, very thinly sliced

To serve
soy sauce
wasabi

1. Season the rice to taste with the sushi rice seasoning.

2. Place 2 of the seaweed sheets on to a board. Spread a quarter of the rice over each, cover with the smoked salmon, then the cucumber. Spoon over the remaining rice, then top with the other seaweed sheets. Press the sushi down well so the layers stick together.

3. Cut into 4 triangles and serve with soy and wasabi.

Lindon Potted Crab

Tolkien thought of Middle-earth as a kind of other-Europe – a Europe of a mythologized time and dimension long before – and outside of – the present day. The famous map of Middle-earth was, to some degree, calqued on that of Europe, with The Shire, for example, corresponding to the English West Midlands and Minas Tirith to Mediterranean Rome. But what of Beleriand, the Elvish lands of the First Age that, at the close of *The Silmarillion*, are largely submerged beneath the ocean but whose remnants – Forlindon and Harlindon – lie, at the time of the events of *The Lord of the Rings*, to the west of the Shire, north and south of the Gulf of Lune? The geography of Lindon strongly recalls that of Wales and the south-west of England, deeply divided by the Bristol Channel, while the lost land of Beleriand may refer to the lost lands of Lyonesse, off the Cornish coast – in legend swallowed by the ocean in a single night – as well as to the sunken kingdom of Cantre'r Gwaelod, in Wales's Cardigan Bay.

Just like the palimpsest geography of Middle-earth, this simple recipe, made from fresh crab meat, recalls at once the wild, rocky coastline of Lindon and that of Cornwall and Wales.

— ··—

This crab pâté is very versatile: for speedy but impressive canapés, you can serve it on mini blinis – Russian-style pancakes – or for a dinner-party starter, pile it into individual ramekins and serve with wholemeal toast triangles and lemon wedges to squeeze over.

Serves 4–6
Prep time 10 minutes

30–36 ready-made cocktail-sized blinis
275 g (9 oz) white crab meat
125 g (4 oz) cream cheese
1–2 teaspoons sweet chilli sauce, to taste (optional)
2–3 teaspoons lemon juice, to taste
salt and pepper
snipped chives or coriander, to garnish (optional)

1. Wrap the blinis in foil and warm them in a preheated oven, 180°C (350°F), Gas Mark 4, or according to the packet instructions.

2. Meanwhile, add the remaining ingredients to a bowl and mash with a fork to the desired consistency. (This can be done in a food processor if you wish.) Season to taste.

3. Serve the pâté with the warmed blinis, garnishing with the chives, if desired.

Elwing's White Pizza

Eärendil's (see page 58) wife is the Half-elven princess Elwing, whose name means 'Star-foam' and who was called 'The White'. Her story strongly recalls the many human–animal metamorphoses found in Greek mythology and seems to have been in part inspired by Ovid's tale of Ceyx and Alcyone in *Metamorphoses*. During her husband's absence at sea, Elwing is left in possession of one of the Silmarils and, to escape the sons of Fëanor who come in search of it, she throws herself off a headland, but is transformed into a great white seabird. In this form, she flies over the ocean to be reunited with her husband. Tolkien does not tell us which type of bird she becomes, but from the description we might imagine a large gull or an albatross, a bird often revered by sailors.

This beautiful pizza, white with mozzarella, is our tribute to this courageous heroine.

For a super-speedy lunch or supper, build your own pizza without the faff, using ready-made pizza bases. Use this recipe as a template and then get as creative as you like by varying the toppings. Good choices include olives, anchovies, capers, passata, chillies, sliced peppers and mushrooms, ham, blue cheese and pepperoni.

Serves 4
Prep + cook time 15 minutes

4 ready-made mini pizza bases
2 garlic cloves, halved
250 g (8 oz) mozzarella cheese,
  shredded
150 g (5 oz) prosciutto, sliced
50 g (2 oz) rocket leaves
balsamic vinegar, to taste
salt and pepper

1. Rub the top surfaces of the pizza bases with the cut faces of the garlic cloves.

2. Put the pizza bases on a baking sheet, top with the mozzarella and bake in a preheated oven, 200°C (400°F), Gas Mark 6, for 10 minutes until the bases are golden.

3. Top the pizzas with slices of prosciutto and rocket leaves, season to taste with salt and pepper and a drizzle of balsamic vinegar and serve immediately.

Fingolfin's Salt Cod Fritters

Fëanor's desire for revenge against Morgoth, who has stolen the Elf-smith's most prized creation, the Silmarils (see pages 25, 61 and 120), leads to the Kinslaying at Alqualondë and the subsequent Flight of the Noldor from Valinor. While Fëanor and his sons steal away in the ships of the Teleri to pursue Morgoth to Middle-earth, his kindred, led by his half-brother Fingolfin, have to make the journey by trekking across the frozen seas in the far north, the Helcaraxë – a journey of great hardship that leads to the death of many, including Fingolfin's wife.

It is hard not to imagine Fingolfin and his people as like the early Vikings exploring and settling the northern reaches of the Atlantic, as far, it seems, as Newfoundland (though their preferred transportation method, of course, was the ship). One of the Vikings' staple foods that they took to sustain them in out-of-the-way places was dried fish – harðfiskur in Icelandic – which was preserved by being dried on open-air wooden racks and which could last for several years. Perhaps Fingolfin and his people, too, took their supplies with them and from time to time comforted themselves with a heartening dish like this one before they faced the next stage of their gruelling journey into exile and uncertainty.

continued overleaf ⇨

With a crispy coating and the insides fluffy and with juicy pieces of salt cod, these are delicious served piping hot with aperitifs or as a starter. Serve with lemon wedges for squeezing over and, for an extra-indulgent treat, perhaps a bowl of creamy garlic mayo for dipping.

Serves 4
Prep + cook time 50 minutes, plus soaking and standing

250 g (8 oz) piece of salt cod
400 g (13 oz) potatoes, peeled and
  quartered
1 shallot, grated
1 egg yolk
1 bunch of parsley, chopped
plain flour, for dusting
vegetable oil, for deep-frying
salt
lemon wedges, to serve

1. Soak the salt cod in cold water in the refrigerator for 24–48 hours, depending on its thickness, changing the water at least twice. Drain, then place the fish in a saucepan and cover with fresh cold water. Heat just to boiling point, then remove the pan from the heat and leave to stand for 15 minutes.

2. Meanwhile, cook the potatoes in a separate saucepan of lightly salted boiling water for 15 minutes until tender. Drain well, then return to the pan and mash until smooth. Drain the salt cod, discard any skin and bones, then flake into small pieces. Squeeze away any excess water from the shallot. Stir the salt cod, shallot, egg yolk and parsley into the mashed potato. Using your hands, form the mixture into about 16 small egg shapes and dust all over with flour.

3. Pour the oil into a large, deep saucepan or deep fat-fryer to a depth of at least 7 cm (3 inches) and heat to 180–190°C (350–375°F), or until a cube of bread browns in 30 seconds. Deep-fry the croquettes in 2 or 3 batches for about 3 minutes, until golden, then remove with a slotted spoon. Drain on kitchen paper and keep warm while you cook the remaining croquettes.

4. Serve warm with lemon wedges for squeezing over.

Legolas's Duck in Lettuce Boats

In *The Lord of the Rings*, the Lord of Lothlórien, Celeborn, equips the Fellowship with three Elvish boats to aid their journey south, along the Silverlode (see page 48) and then on down the Great River towards Gondor. Tolkien describes the boats as made out of a grey wood but very light and propelled with short paddles with leaflike blades – and as rather hard to steer, even if remarkably buoyant. It's a description that might make us think of the wicker-and-hide-covered boats of ancient Britain and Ireland – the Irish corrach and Welsh coracle – fragile boats that the early wandering saints of the islands were said to sail in as they went from community to community spreading the word of God.

Our Eastern-inspired dish here uses lettuce-leaf coracles in which to float lightly spiced spoonfuls of duck – a bird that, incidentally, would probably have flourished along the reedy banks of the Anduin and which the expert marksman Legolas could easily have hunted with his bow. Some of the other ingredients he might have found it harder to come by, though!

The essential ingredient in this sticky and fragrant hot duck salad is Chinese five spice, a warming mix of fennel, clove, star anise, cassia and ginger. For a more substantial meal, serve the duck over a tangle of egg noodles, perhaps with steamed pak choi on the side.

Serves 4
Prep + cook time 30 minutes

2 tablespoons sesame oil

2 duck breasts, about 175 g (6 oz) each, cut into thin strips

2 teaspoons Chinese five spice powder

2 tablespoons dark soy sauce

2 tablespoons clear honey

2 tablespoons toasted sesame seeds

8 Little Gem lettuce leaves

To garnish
4 spring onions, finely chopped
1 small carrot, peeled and grated

1. Heat the oil in a heavy-based frying pan. Toss the duck strips with the Chinese five spice powder in a bowl, then fry over a high heat for 8–10 minutes until cooked and crispy. Add the soy sauce and honey and cook for a further 2 minutes to coat in the sticky glaze. Scatter with the sesame seeds and keep warm.

2. Wash and pat dry the lettuce leaves and place on a serving board. Place spoonfuls of the duck into the leaves, then garnish each with the spring onions and carrot.

Vingilótë Pasties

The Half-elven Eärendil – father of Elrond and Elros – is the saviour-like figure of the Elves and Men of Beleriand who sails to Valinor to seek the aid of the Valar in their struggle against Morgoth in Middle-earth. He was, in fact, the first figure Tolkien imagined in his evolving mythos – whose origins lie at the outbreak of the First World War when Europe was rushing headlong into destruction. In Tolkien's poem relating the story of the voyage of 'Éarendel', the hero becomes the Evening and Morning Star, a symbol of hope and resurrection.

Eärendil's ship is Vingilótë, which, under Círdan's guidance, he makes out of white beechwood and rigs with silver sails. Moved by the plight of the Elves and Men, the Valar accept his plea and launch an all-out war on Morgoth. They hallow Eärendil's ship and raise it into the air and, with one of the Silmarils displayed on his brow, the Half-elven pilot takes part in the final great battle – the War of Wrath – slaying the dragon Ancalagon. While Eärendil as the Evening Star and Redeemer has clear associations with Christ, who in Revelations is called the Bright and Morning Star, but Tolkien may also have been thinking of the Greek star constellation Argo Navis ('the Ship Argo'), which commemorated the magical ship of Jason and the Argonauts.

Our boat-shaped pasties here commemorate Vingilótë – we might even imagine Eärendil taking one of these delicious treats on board each night as he makes his journey across the skies.

These little pies, packed with colourful veg, are delicious served warm or cold with a salad. And they are ideal no-cutlery-needed picnic fare too. For a meaty version, omit the peppers and mix 50 g (2 oz) diced ham into the tomato mixture once it has cooled.

Makes 4
Prep + cook time 1 hour

1 tablespoon olive oil
1 onion, chopped
2 garlic cloves, finely chopped
1 courgette, diced
½ yellow pepper, deseeded and diced
½ red pepper, deseeded and diced
400 g (13 oz) can chopped tomatoes
1 tablespoon chopped rosemary or
    basil
½ teaspoon caster sugar
beaten egg, to glaze
salt and pepper

For the pastry
175 g (6 oz) bread flour, plus extra
    for dusting
75 g (3 oz) butter, diced
75 g (3 oz) mature Cheddar cheese,
    diced, plus extra, grated, for
    sprinkling
2 egg yolks
2 teaspoons water

1. Heat the oil in a saucepan, add the onion and fry for 5 minutes until softened. Add the garlic, courgette and diced peppers and fry briefly, then add the tomatoes, herbs, sugar and a little salt and pepper. Simmer, uncovered, for 10 minutes, stirring from time to time until thickened. Cool.

2. Make the pastry. Add the flour, butter and a little salt and pepper to a bowl, rub in the butter with your fingertips until you have fine crumbs, then stir in the cheese. Add the egg yolks and water and mix to form a smooth dough.

3. Knead lightly on a lightly floured surface, then cut the dough into 4 pieces. Roll one of the pieces out between 2 sheets of clingfilm, patting into a neat shape until you have an 18 cm (7 inch) circle. Remove the top sheet of clingfilm, spoon one-quarter of the filling in the centre, brush the pastry edges with beaten egg, then fold the pastry circle in half while still on the lower piece of clingfilm.

4. Peel the pastry off the film, lift on to an oiled baking sheet, press the edges together well and press together any breaks in the pastry. Repeat with the remaining pastry pieces and filling until 4 pies have been made.

5. Brush with beaten egg, sprinkle with a little extra cheese and bake in a preheated oven, 190°C (375°F), Gas Mark 5, for 20 minutes until golden brown. Loosen and transfer to a wire rack.

Blue Wizard Steaks

One of the great, unsolved mysteries of Tolkien's legendarium is what becomes of the two blue-robed Istari – Wizards – who, unlike Gandalf, Saruman and Radagast – wander into the east of Middle-earth. In Valinor, the Maia Alatar was in the service of Oromë, as probably was his friend, Pallando, so it may have been perfectly natural for them to explore the eastern regions, the old haunts of their master, the Huntsman, himself. Tolkien was somewhat cagey about their fate – hinting that they may have failed, like Saruman, in their mission and became the founder of obscure cults. We prefer to think, however, that they remained faithful, fighting the part of the Free Peoples of Middle-earth at Sauron's back door. They also took care of Oromë's 'sun-cattle' (page 43) and treated themselves to the occasional Kine of Araw steak.

When you're after a quick but delicious lunch, these succulent steaks with their chilli-spiked sauce are just the thing. All you need to serve alongside is a crisp green salad, or if you fancy something a bit heartier, some new potatoes or a few chips.

Serves 4
Prep + cook time 20 minutes

2 tablespoons olive oil

4 fillet steaks, about 175 g
 (6 oz) each

2 tablespoons balsamic vinegar

75 ml (3 fl oz) full-bodied red wine

4 tablespoons beef stock

2 garlic cloves, chopped

1 teaspoon crushed fennel seeds

1 tablespoon sun-dried tomato purée

½ teaspoon crushed dried chillies

salt and pepper

chopped flat-leaf parsley, to garnish

1. Heat the oil in a non-stick frying pan until smoking hot, add the steaks and cook over a very high heat for about 2 minutes on each side, if you want your steaks to be medium rare. For well-done steaks cook for 4–5 minutes on each side. Remove from the pan, season with salt and pepper and keep warm.

2. Pour the vinegar, wine and stock into the pan and boil for 30 seconds, scraping any sediment from the base of the pan. Add the garlic and fennel seeds, then whisk in the sun-dried tomato purée and crushed chillies. Bring the sauce to the boil, then boil fast to reduce down until syrupy.

3. Transfer the steaks to serving plates, pouring any collected meat juices into the sauce. Return the sauce to the boil, then season with salt and pepper.

4. Slice the steaks before serving, if you wish. Pour the sauce over the steaks and serve immediately, garnished with chopped parsley.

Fëanor's Fiery Pumpkin Bake

Fëanor is one of the lead characters of *The Silmarillion* – a hot-headed, proud Noldorin Elf-prince who is the Elves' greatest craftsman and smith. In type, he is similar to the 'culture heroes' found in many real-world mythologies – like Prometheus in Greek mythology or Coyote in Native American myths – heroes who defy the gods in order to bring new or forbidden technologies into the world. Fëanor creates not only the Silmarils – the transcendently beautiful gems that are the leitmotif of *The Silmarillion* – but also the Tengwar script – of which we find examples in *The Hobbit* and *The Lord of the Rings*.

Like Prometheus, the jewel-smith Fëanor is closely associated with fire – even his name means 'Spirit of Fire'. His fiery temperament brings disaster to his people, the Noldor, who, because of his pride and embittered desire for revenge, must live in exile in Middle-earth. This oven-baked dish, with its jewel-like colours and mouth-tingling heat, is the perfect commemoration of this gifted but flawed hero of the First Age.

⌐—··⌐

Earthy beetroot and sweet pumpkin contrast beautifully with the creamy, tangy goats' cheese in this one-tin vegetarian dish. It requires hardly any hands-on time so is ideal for a light midweek supper. The beetroot will stain your hands so you may want to wear rubber gloves when peeling and chopping it.

Serves 4
Prep + cook time 50 minutes

400 g (13 oz) raw beetroot, peeled and diced

625 g (1¼ lb) pumpkin or butternut squash, peeled, deseeded and cut into slightly larger dice than the beetroot

1 red onion, cut into wedges

2 tablespoons olive oil

2 teaspoons fennel seeds

½ teaspoon chipotle chilli flakes

2 small goats' cheeses, 100 g (3½ oz) each

salt and pepper

chopped rosemary, to garnish

1. Put the vegetables into a roasting tin, drizzle with the oil and sprinkle with the fennel seeds, chilli flakes and salt and pepper. Roast in a preheated oven, 200°C (400°F), Gas Mark 6, for 20–25 minutes, turning once, until well browned and tender.

2. Cut the goats' cheeses into thirds and nestle among the roasted vegetables. Sprinkle the cheeses with a little salt and pepper and drizzle with some of the pan juices.

3. Return the dish to the oven and cook for about 5 minutes until the cheese is just beginning to melt. Sprinkle with rosemary and serve immediately.

Lúthien's Asparagus Tart

The story of the mortal Beren and the Elf-maid Lúthien is one of the central stories of Tolkien's legendarium – a tale told in *The Silmarillion* but also told in brief by Aragorn to Frodo in *The Lord of the Rings*. They are archetypal lovers like Tristan and Isolde or Orpheus and Eurydice, with whose stories theirs has some striking resemblances, and their enduring love, against all the odds – a resistant father, a vengeful dark lord and even death itself – prefigures that of their descendants Aragorn and Arwen in Tolkien's epic novel.

For Tolkien, Lúthien was also an idealization and commemoration of his own great love, his wife, Edith, who is even called by that name on the Tolkiens' shared gravestone in Wolvercote Cemetery, Oxford, just as the writer is called Beren. In Tolkien's stories, Lúthien is the most beautiful of the Elves and is closely associated with the spring – flowers bloom beneath her feet as she passes and her voice is said to melt away the winter's ice and cold. What better dish, then, to honour Tolkien's heroine than a tart made from asparagus, whose tender, green shoots appear all too briefly in the springtime.

⌐—···—⌐

Serve this delicious asparagus tart hot topped with Parmesan shavings and rocket leaves or – for a pretty-as-a-picture tart – allow to cool and scatter over a handful of edible flowers. Look out for edible flower mixes, including cornflowers, pansies and nasturtiums, in the chilled vegetable aisle of big supermarkets.

Serves 2
Prep + cook time 25 minutes

125 g (4 oz) asparagus spears, trimmed
½ x 375 g (12 oz) sheet of ready-rolled puff pastry
1 tablespoon ready-made pesto
4 cherry tomatoes, halved

To serve (optional)
Parmesan cheese shavings
rocket leaves
balsamic glaze
edible flowers

1. Cook the asparagus in a saucepan of lightly salted boiling water for 2 minutes. Drain and rinse under cold water, then drain again.

2. Place the pastry on a baking sheet. Spread the pesto evenly over the pastry, leaving a 1 cm (½ inch) border around the edge. Arrange the asparagus on the pesto. Place the tomatoes on top.

3. Bake in a preheated oven, 200°C (400°F), Gas Mark 6, for 15–20 minutes until the pastry is crisp and golden. Serve warm with Parmesan cheese shavings, rocket leaves and a drizzle of balsamic syrup or at room temperature, scattered with edible flowers.

Gardens of Lórien Avocado

Avocados are so commonplace today – served on sourdough for breakfast and, spiked with coriander and chili, as guacamole – that it is easy to forget their origins in ancient Mesoamerica. European conquistadors first tasted, and indeed liked them in the sixteenth century, but it would only be in the late twentieth that they reached European supermarkets in any great quantity. Since then they have become every hipster's superfood.

If avocados were met with wonder and mirth in 1970s suburbia, imagine how they might be viewed in Third Age Gondorian Minas Tirith, let alone Edoras, the Anglo-Saxon-style, wooden-built capital of Rohan. They simply have no place in the cuisines of Middle-earth. Perhaps, though, we could find a place for them in Aman, Tolkien's American-like continent, far across the Sundering Seas – luxuriantly growing in the Gardens of Lórien in Valinor and supped upon by those highest of High Elves, the Vanya – golden-haired, 'angelheaded hipsters' if ever there were.

───··──

Heart-healthy, nutrient-dense avocado is the star of the show in this simple, fresh-tasting guacamole recipe. Serve with strips of toasted pitta bread or tortilla chips, or – keeping with the healthy theme – with oatcakes and vegetable crudités, such as cucumber, peppers and carrots.

Serves 4
Prep time 10 minutes

2 avocados, peeled, stoned
   and chopped
juice of 1 lime
6 cherry tomatoes, diced
1 tablespoon chopped coriander leaves
1–2 garlic cloves, crushed

1. Put the avocados and lime juice in a bowl and mash together to prevent discoloration, then stir in the remaining ingredients.

2. Serve immediately.

Dining in Valinor

Tolkien's classification of the Elves is highly complex – in part reflecting the strong sense of identity that his Elves themselves possessed. Not only do they seem to have a fierce pride regarding their kindred – Teleri, Noldor or Vanyar – but they were also sharply aware of the decisive division between those who have been to Aman ('the blessed realm') and seen the light of the Two Trees – the Caliquendi ('Elves of the Light') – and those who have not – the Moriquendi ('Elves of Darkness') either because they refuse outright to heed the summons of the Valar (the Avari) and because, for various reasons, they turn aside from the journey – the Úmanyar ('those not of Aman').

On Tolkien's Arda ('Earth'), Aman was originally a continent situated to the west of Middle-earth, across the great sea Belegaer. Although it is the home of the immortal Valar and Maiar – Tolkien's greater and lesser powers – and many of the likewise immortal Elves and is hence known as the Undying Lands, it is a 'real', physical place, with its own geography, flora and fauna, just like Middle-earth. At the end of the Second Age, after the downfall of Númenor and the catastrophic Changing of Arda from flat to spherical, the continent of Aman is removed from the world altogether, reachable only by the Elves (and a few others) by sailing along the Straight Road, half on the sea, half in the sky.

By this cosmological account, Aman cannot be the Americas – which in any case physically differ from the continent of the Valar. Nonetheless, Tolkien's conception of Aman was undoubtedly influenced by the Americas, which in the first centuries after their 'discovery' by Europeans in 1492 were described in terms of an earthly paradise, as a promised land of peace and plenty. Tolkien's descriptions of Valinor – the land of the Valar in Aman – with the Two Trees stretching towards heaven and the Eden-like Gardens of Lórien – may remind us of Christopher Columbus's hyperbolic description (1493) of the island of Hispaniola with its 'most lofty mountains [...]; all most beautiful in a thousand shapes, and all accessible, and full of trees of a thousand kinds, [where] the nightingale was singing, and other birds of a thousand sorts.' This description, and many others like it in later decades, struck a chord in a Europe torn by war and want, helping to fuel wave after wave of immigration and colonial settlement. In Tolkien's legendarium, Aman has a similar resonance as a 'land of milk and honey' among the peoples of Middle-earth, especially, of course, the Elves, who feel an unceasing urge to sail west across the sea to the utopia of their hearts.

So far and throughout the rest of this recipe book, then, we have imagined an Aman that is both like and unlike America, offering foodstuffs that, strictly speaking, are impossible in Middle-earth but conceivable in Aman; all the New World produce that we take for granted today – potatoes, tomatoes, avocados, blueberries, pumpkins and so on. (Tolkien took similar liberties with the logic of his world, allowing both the potato and tobacco plant to feature prominently in his Middle-earth, 'Old World' flora, so we feel no qualms!) On this basis we have evolved something of an Amanian cuisine, imagining the foods and drink of the Elves of Aman and and even, on occasion, dining with the Valar themselves.

Main Meals

Everyone is for ever hungry in *The Hobbit* – whether they're the title character, a Dwarf, a Wizard, a Spider, a Goblin, a Dragon ... or even an Elf. The characters and the monsters they meet all seem to have food on the brain and are always wondering about their next meal. In part, this is because *The Hobbit* is a children's book – kids love reading about food (though, to be honest, don't we all?), and partly because Bilbo Baggins – true to Hobbit-kind – is so heavily invested in food and it's his point of view that we are following in the story. In his Hobbit-centric eyes, everyone just has to be thinking of their stomachs.

Nonetheless, we may be a little shocked that the Elves, too, have healthy appetites, especially if we come to *The Hobbit* with certain prejudices nurtured by *The Lord of the Rings* or, especially, by *The Silmarillion*. Aren't they just too ethereal and, well, too fey to have anything so base as an appetite? Yet here in *The Hobbit* we find them, again and again, feasting, guzzling, and, what's more, talking and singing about food ... And not any old food, but proper, stomach-lining, heavy-duty food – faggots and bannocks and rich red wine.

In this section, then, you will find dishes, hearty ones as well as more refined ones, that might especially satisfy the Elves as Tolkien portrayed them in *The Hobbit*. We don't imagine, though, that the Elves of Beleriand or Lothlórien would turn their nose up at them either.

Eregion Root Vegetable Stew

We have named this tasty, comforting stew for the Noldor kingdom of Eregion which lies just to the west of the Misty Mountains and the Dwarvish realm of Moria. It is here that, during the Second Age, Sauron tricks the Elven jewel-smiths – the Gwaith-i-Mírdain, led by Celebrimbor, grandson of Fëanor (page 61) – into forging the Rings of Power (page 79). In *The Lord of the Rings* the Fellowship pass through the region, but it has been destroyed many hundreds of years before – one of the many ruined or wasted kingdoms, Elven, Dwarven and Dúnedain, that haunt Tolkien's Middle-earth. It is almost as if he is conjuring up 'Dark Age' Britain – its hills scattered with the melancholy ruins of its Roman past.

While in Eregion, the Fellowship may well have eaten this stew, made from gathered roots, while sitting under the ruins of Celebrimbor's guild-house where, long before, the Rings of Power were made.

⌒ ⋯ ⌒

Comfort in a steaming bowl, this is what you'll want to eat after a brisk walk on a cold day. It freezes well so you can double up the quantities and make a big batch.

Serves 4
Prep + cook time 1½ hours

100 g (3½ oz) pearl barley
2 tablespoons olive oil
1 large onion, finely chopped
2 leeks, trimmed, cleaned and finely
   chopped
1 celery stick, finely chopped
750 g (1½ lb) mixed root vegetables
   such as parsnips, swede, turnips,
   carrots and potatoes, evenly diced
1.2 litres (2 pints) vegetable stock
1 bouquet garni
salt and pepper

1. Bring a large saucepan of water to the boil and pour in the pearl barley. Cook at a gentle simmer for 30 minutes. Drain well.

2. Meanwhile, heat the oil in a large, heavy-based saucepan over a medium-low heat, add the onion, leeks and celery and fry gently for 8–10 minutes or until softened but not coloured. Add the root vegetables and cook for a further 5 minutes, stirring regularly.

3. Pour in the stock, add the bouquet garni and bring to the boil. Stir in the pearl barley, then reduce the heat and simmer for 25–30 minutes or until the vegetables and pearl barley are tender. Remove the bouquet garni and season to taste with salt and pepper. Ladle into bowls and serve.

Vanyar Haricot Bean Stew

Tolkien depicts Valinor – part New World, part paradise – as a land of plenty. Its characteristic landscape is the garden, nature perfected and preened – as exemplified by the Gardens of Lórien, somewhere to the south of the land. Lórien appears to be largely ornamental – with flowers and trees grown, above all, for their soothing beauty – though we can imagine that the Vanyar – the 'Fair Elves' who live in Valinor – kept practical kitchen gardens, too. As New World Elves, we might think of them as something like Mesoamerican peoples who for hundreds of years before the European conquest tilled the land to produce the classic trio of crops – the 'three sisters' of corn, squash and beans.

It takes a lot of work to tend to paradise, and this quick-and-easy bean stew would have been a welcome dish for any Vanyar, king or subject, after a hard day's work in the garden.

***

This vegan bean stew is a real winter warmer and very budget-friendly. You can vary the beans, depending on what's in your store cupboard – borlotti beans and butter beans work especially well. Serve with crusty bread or spooned over baked potatoes.

Serves 4
Prep + cook time 30 minutes

3 tablespoons olive oil
1 small onion, chopped
2 garlic cloves, finely chopped
2 carrots, peeled and diced
1 tablespoon rosemary, leaves picked
  and chopped
2 x 400 g (13 oz) cans haricot beans,
  rinsed and drained
600 ml (1 pint) vegetable stock
salt and pepper

1. Heat the olive oil in a large, heavy-based frying pan and cook the onion, garlic, carrots and rosemary over a medium heat, stirring occasionally, for 3–4 minutes until softened.

2. Add the haricot beans and vegetable stock and bring to the boil. Simmer briskly, uncovered, for 10 minutes until piping hot, then carefully scoop out a third of the beans.

3. Place in a food processor and whizz until smooth. Return the puréed beans to the pan, stir to combine and heat through. Season to taste, then serve.

Moriquendi Bean & Lentil Curry

The Noldor seem to use the term 'Moriquendi' as an insult to the Avari, perhaps because they refuse outright to heed the summons of the Valar (page 66). Most of the Avari freely return their hostility. Tolkien nowhere suggests that the Avari are evil, though in the early days some were captured, corrupted and bred to become the race of Orcs, who undoubtedly are.

This striking dish of black lentils and beans is our tribute to the Dark Elves – that forgotten, secretive people – its black colours and Eastern flavours evoking the dark forests of the far east of Middle-earth.

This black bean dish really delivers both on flavour and health benefits. It's full of zingy spices and provides plenty of fibre, protein, iron, vitamins and antioxidants. Don't forget to start the prepping the evening before by soaking the lentils.

Serves 4
Prep + cook time 1½ hours,
plus soaking

125 g (4 oz) dried split black lentils, rinsed and drained

500 ml (17 fl oz) boiling water

1 tablespoon groundnut oil

1 onion, finely chopped

3 garlic cloves, crushed

2 teaspoons peeled and finely grated fresh root ginger

2 fresh green chillies, halved lengthways

1 teaspoon each of ground turmeric, paprika, cumin and coriander

1 x 400 g (13 oz) can black beans, rinsed and drained

500 ml (17 fl oz) cold water

200 g (7 oz) baby spinach

large handful of chopped coriander leaves

salt

200 ml (7 fl oz) fat-free natural yogurt, whisked, to serve

1. Place the lentils in a deep bowl and cover with cold water. Leave to soak for 10–12 hours. Transfer to a colander and rinse under cold running water. Drain and place in a medium saucepan with the measured boiling water. Bring to the boil, then reduce the heat to low.

2. Simmer gently for 35–40 minutes, skimming off any scum that rises to the surface and stirring often.

3. Heat the oil in a large saucepan and add the onion, garlic, ginger and chillies. Stir-fry for 5–6 minutes and then add the turmeric, paprika, cumin, ground coriander, black beans and lentils.

4. Add the measured cold water and bring to the boil. Reduce the heat and stir in the spinach. Cook gently for 10–15 minutes, stirring often. Remove from the heat and season with salt to taste. Stir in the chopped coriander and drizzle over the yogurt. Sprinkle with a little paprika and serve immediately.

Gil-galad Golden Dhal

Part of the extraordinary achievement and wonder of Tolkien's Middle-earth is that not only did he create its epic present – the late Third Age as presented in the novels *The Hobbit* and *The Lord of the Rings* – but also its mythological history and hinterland, a distant heroic age – the First and Second Ages – as found in *The Silmarillion* and elsewhere. This gives his work a sense of grandeur and depth that makes it comparable with the great 'national' epics that so inspired him – from Homer's *Iliad* to the Anglo-Saxon 'Beowulf', which similarly look back to a golden age of larger-than-life heroes.

Looming large in the pantheon of the Second Age is Gil-galad – 'Star of Radiance' – the last High King of the Elves who defeats Sauron but is himself slain in their struggle. In the Third Age he remains a figure of hope and resilience and appears in *The Lord of the Rings* as a mythic hero, the subject of song and tale – most notably when Sam recalls the opening verses of a heroic song about him, as taught to him by Bilbo as a boy: 'Gil-galad was an elven-king …'

The golden colour of this dish is symbolic of the golden memory of this last great Elven King, as he rides with his troops against Sauron, shields and banners raised high.

This works as a vegan main course – spoon over some thick dairy-free yogurt with a little spicy harissa paste stirred through and with toasted flatbreads alongside – or as side dish for grilled or roasted meat and poultry.

Serves 2
Prep + cook time 45 minutes

2 tablespoons olive oil

2 onions, finely chopped

4 garlic cloves, finely chopped

2 teaspoons ground turmeric

2 teaspoons ground fenugreek

225 g (7½ oz) dried yellow lentils, rinsed and drained

1 x 400 g (13 oz) can chopped tomatoes

2 teaspoons sugar

750 ml (1¼ pints) water

small bunch of coriander, finely chopped

salt and pepper

1. Heat the oil in the base of a large, heavy-based saucepan over a medium heat, stir in the onions and garlic and cook for 2–3 minutes to soften a little. Add the turmeric, fenugreek and lentils and stir to coat well, then stir in the tomatoes and sugar.

2. Pour in the measured water and bring to the boil, then reduce the heat, cover and cook gently for about 30 minutes until the lentils are tender but not mushy, adding a little more water if necessary. Stir in half the coriander and season with salt and pepper. Serve garnished with the remaining coriander.

Cuiviénen Mussels

The Awakening of the Elves takes place in the far east of Middle-earth, in the forests around the Bay of Cuiviénen, part of the Inland Sea of Helcar. The event is briefly described in *The Silmarillion*, but was also the subject of a late, somewhat curious work of Tolkien's known as 'The Cuivienyarna'. This is essentially what purports to be a piece of archaic Elven lore describing the exponential increase in the number of Elves after the initial awakening of pairs of Elves, prosaically named in Quena 'First', 'Second' and 'Third' – the forefathers and foremothers of the Vanyar, Noldor and Teleri.

Over time the Elves learn by a process of trial and error the rudiments of culture – language, poetry, song, certainly; shelter and clothing; and fire for warmth and, no doubt, cooking. Perhaps, as these childlike Elves wandered on the seashore of Helcar looking in wonder at the new world they found themselves in, they gathered mussels from the rocks. Later they may have cooked them simply with herbs, rather as in this recipe, though wine, admittedly, was probably still some way away along the Elves' evolutionary path.

Food doesn't have to be complicated; sometimes a simple one-pot meal is just right – this French classic is a great example. Serve with fresh crusty bread to mop up every last drop of the wine and garlic-scented cooking juices.

Serves 4
Prep + cook time 15 minutes

2 tablespoons olive oil

2 garlic cloves, sliced

1.5 kg (3 lb) live mussels, scrubbed
  and debearded

200 ml (7 fl oz) dry white wine

handful of flat-leaf parsley, chopped

1. Heat the oil in a large saucepan. Add the garlic and cook for 30 seconds until lightly golden. Add the mussels, discarding any that are cracked or don't shut when tapped, and the wine.

2. Cover the pan and cook for 5 minutes, shaking the pan occasionally, or until the mussels have opened. Discard any that remain closed.

3. Stir in the parsley and serve immediately.

Isle of Balar Grilled Lobster

In the First Age the Isle of Balar lies to the south of Beleriand, in the Bay of Balar, Christopher Tolkien's map of Beleriand showing it as a leaflike island with low-lying mountains at its southern tip. According to the tales of the Elves, it was a fragment of Tol Eressëa, the floating island that Ulmo used to bring the Eldar to Aman (page 45). During the Wars of Beleriand, it becomes a refuge for Elves escaping the devastation – both Noldor from Gondolin (page 31) and the Falathrim of Círdan (page 21). It also becomes home to havens from which the Elves send out ships to seek the aid of the Valar, including Eärendil's Vingilot.

The refugees no doubt depended on the sea to feed themselves. The coastal-dwelling Falathrim would have been very used to the diet on offer, but the rather spoiled Elves of Gondolin much less so. Perhaps the delicious lobster dish here would have tempted the Noldor to try something new, though.

—··—

This stunning-looking dish is surprisingly easy to make and a luxurious choice for a special occasion. Serve with a green salad dressed with a sharp lemony vinaigrette to cut through the rich flavours and perhaps some crusty bread for soaking up the creamy sauce.

Serves 4
Prep + cook time 25 minutes

100 g (3 oz) butter, softened
1 garlic clove, crushed
1 tablespoon lemon juice
large handful of chopped parsley
large handful of chopped chives
2 cooked lobsters
salt and pepper

To serve
green salad with fennel
potato wedges

1. Mix together the butter, garlic, lemon juice and herbs and season. Place in a sheet of clingfilm, roll into a cylinder and twist the ends to seal. Put in the freezer for 5 minutes to harden a little.

2. Snap the claws away from the lobsters and crack the shell with the back of a heavy knife to remove the meat inside.

3. Cut each lobster body in half lengthways. Wash out the head cavities with cold water and divide the claw meat between them.

4. Put the lobsters on a grill pan, cut side up, slice the butter and place on top. Cook under a preheated hot grill for 5–7 minutes until bubbling. Serve with green salad and potato wedges.

Lauterbrunnen Trout

O ne of the inspirations for Rivendell – the refuge of the Elves nestled in a secret valley in the foothills of the Misty Mountains – is the Lauterbrunnental in Switzerland, an idyllic 'trough', or steep-sided, Alpine valley in the canton of Bern famous for its springs and waterfalls. Tolkien went hiking in the valley as a young man in 1911 and painted watercolours that would later evolve into his depictions – both literary and artistic – of Elrond's green, hidden valley. The name of the river that flows through Rivendell, the Bruinen, or the Loudwater, plays on the Swiss valley's name, which itself seems to mean either 'Many Springs' or 'Loud Springs'.

The streams of the Lauterbrunnental teem with trout – the inspiration for this fresh-tasting dish.

A go-to recipe when you need dinner in a dash, this elegant trout dish is wonderful with some buttered new potatoes and asparagus in spring or with a fresh green salad in summer. And it looks impressive too!

Serves 4–6
Prep + cook time 30 minutes

3 tablespoons olive oil
1.5 kg (3 lb) thick piece of trout,
  cut into 2 fillets
1 lemon, sliced
handful of mixed herbs, finely chopped
salt

For the tartare
6 tablespoons mayonnaise
2 teaspoons drained capers, roughly
  chopped
1 spring onion, chopped
1 teaspoon caster sugar
1 teaspoon wholegrain mustard
lemon juice, to taste
handful of dill, chopped

1. Brush a large baking sheet with a little of the oil. Place 1 trout fillet, skin-side down, on the prepared sheet and season with a little salt. Top with the lemon slices and herbs. Season the other fillet and place on top, skin-side up.

2. Tie pieces of kitchen string around the trout to secure. Drizzle over the remaining oil. Place in a preheated oven, 220°C (425°F), Gas Mark 7, for 25 minutes or until just cooked through.

3. Meanwhile, mix together the tartare ingredients and place in a serving bowl. Serve the fish with the tartare alongside.

Stuffed Bream with Samphire

At the end of the First Age most of the Elvish lands of Beleriand are destroyed and submerged by the sea, leaving just the area known as Lindon beside the Grey Mountains. Some of the hills survive as small islands off Lindon's coast in the Great Sea Belegaer, including Himling, or Himring, on which once stood the fortress of Maedhros, eldest son of Fëanor.

These islands must have been sad enough places, reminders of long-lost realms and heroes. Perhaps sometimes, in the Second Age, Elves and Númenórean Men disembarked on these Western Isles to mull upon their ancient past and kindred. Perhaps, too, they sometimes tarried on the seashores, fishing and gathering samphire from the shingle, so as to make a fine supper for themselves as they watched the sun set down over the Belegaer.

—···—

Samphire is a sea vegetable that grows along the shoreline and in marshes. You can find it at fishmongers and bigger supermarkets. Crunchy and salty, it's the ideal partner for fish and works really well with the satisfyingly meaty texture of these stuffed bream fillets.

Serves 4
Prep + cook time 1 hour 20 minutes

750 g (1½ lb) Maris Piper or other floury potatoes, thinly sliced
6 tablespoons olive oil
1 tablespoon chopped thyme
4 bream fillets, about 150 g (5 oz) each
75 g (3 oz) prosciutto, chopped
2 shallots, finely chopped
finely grated rind of 1 lemon
200 g (7 oz) samphire
salt and pepper

1. Toss the potato slices with 4 tablespoons of the oil, a little salt and pepper and the thyme in a bowl. Tip into a roasting tin or ovenproof dish and spread out in an even layer. Cover with foil and bake in a preheated oven, 190°C (375°F), Gas Mark 5, for about 30 minutes until the potatoes are tender.

2. Score the bream fillets with a sharp knife. Mix the prosciutto with the shallots, lemon rind and a little pepper and use to sandwich the bream fillets together. Tie at intervals with string. Cut each of the sandwiched fillets through the centre to make 4 even-sized portions.

3. Lay the fish over the potatoes and return to the oven, uncovered, for a further 20 minutes or until the fish is cooked through.

4. Scatter the samphire around the fish and drizzle with the remaining oil. Return to the oven for a further 5 minutes before serving.

The Three Rings

The 'golden age' of the Elves is the Age of the Stars and, despite the wars and eventual ruin of Beleriand, the First Age, when Elvish culture and civilization are at their height. Subsequent ages in Middle-earth see the dispersal of the Elves across the west of the continent, the diminishment of Elvish power, and the departure of many of the Elves across the sea to Aman. Through these ages the Elves are acutely conscious that, as a people, they are waning and that their 'time' is drawing to a close, even as the 'dominion' of Men is correspondingly rising. It is in this context, Tolkien suggests, that we should see the forging of the Three Rings – Vilya, Narya and Nenya – by Celebrimbor in the Second Age – as an ultimately doomed attempt to enable the leaders of the Elves to artificially preserve and sustain Elvish power and beauty.

In the following three recipes we have matched the Three Rings with three curries, each of whose vivid flavours captures something of the ring's character. They might be just the inspiration you need as you and your fellow diners conspire to combine your powers to overthrow the Dark Lord and destroy the influence of the One Ring.

Nenya – Cod & Coconut Curry

The preserving power of the Three Rings is best seen in the Nenya, the Ring of Water, with its adamant (diamond) set into a band of the silver-like mithril. This is wielded by Galadriel, who uses it to encircle the woodland realm of Lothlórien, which in some sense is removed from time and exists in a state of perpetual flourishing. With the destruction of the One Ring, Nenya loses its power and Lothlórien slowly withers. Here the silver-white of Galadriel's ring is expressed in this vibrant creamy curry, whose whiteness is heightened by the forest green of the lime and coriander leaves.

From tying on your apron to putting on the table in under half an hour, this recipe will be a go-to when you need a midweek meal that is speedy and delicious. All it needs is some basmati or brown rice to go alongside. You can replace the cod with any firm white fish.

Serves 4
Prep + cook time 20 minutes

1 tablespoon groundnut oil
2 teaspoons ground cumin
2 teaspoons ground coriander
2 green chillies, deseeded and sliced
1 cinnamon stick
1 star anise
6 kaffir lime leaves
400 ml (14 fl oz) can coconut milk
4 skinless cod loins, about 150 g
   (5 oz) each
juice of 1 lime
fresh coriander leaves, to garnish
   (optional)

1. Heat the oil in a saucepan, add the spices and lime leaves and cook, stirring, for 2 minutes until fragrant. Pour in the coconut milk and simmer for 5 minutes.

2. Add the fish and simmer for 4–6 minutes until the fish is tender and cooked through. Stir in the lime juice.

3. Sprinkle with coriander leaves, if liked.

Narya – Red Curry

The Red Ring, set with a ruby, is the Ring of Fire. Originally Celebrimbor entrusts the ring to Círdan the Shipwright, but he later relinquishes it to Gandalf to help him in his mission in Middle-earth. Like its companion rings, its chief power is to sustain and preserve, but Círdan, in handing it to Galdalf, also suggests that has the power to inspire resistance and resilience in the face of tyranny. The ring's association with fire seems an appropriate one for a Wizard associated with fireworks, dragons and, ultimately, his combat with a Balrog, or fire-demon. This Thai Red Curry is inspired by the fiery elements of this ring.

Get dinner on the table in half an hour with this speedy one-pan curry that really delivers on exotic Thai flavours. The creamy coconut milk tames the heat of the curry paste and adds depth and balance. All it needs is some freshly cooked jasmine or white rice.

Serves 4
Prep + cook time 35 minutes

1 tablespoon groundnut oil
2–3 tablespoons Thai red curry paste
1 teaspoon ground turmeric
¼ teaspoon ground allspice
500 g (1 lb) lean beef, thinly sliced
400 ml (14 fl oz) coconut milk
250 ml (8 fl oz) beef stock
3 tablespoons Thai fish sauce
50 g (2 oz) palm sugar or brown sugar
4–5 tablespoons tamarind paste
salt and pepper

To garnish
½ red pepper, cut into thin strips
2 spring onions, shredded

1. Heat the oil in a saucepan and stir-fry the curry paste, turmeric and allspice over a medium heat for 3–4 minutes or until fragrant.

2. Add the beef and stir-fry for 4–5 minutes. Add the coconut milk, stock, fish sauce, sugar and tamarind. Reduce the heat and simmer for 10–15 minutes or until the beef is tender. Season to taste and add a little stock or water if the sauce is too dry.

3. Spoon into bowls, garnish with strips of red pepper and spring onion and serve with rice.

Vilya – Pilau Rice

The Blue Ring, a sapphire set in a gold band, initially belongs to Gil-galad, the High King of the Elves through the Second Age, but eventually passes into the hands of Elrond. Like Galadriel, we can assume that Elrond uses the ring's power – it is the greatest of the three – to preserve and protect the realm of Rivendell. The golden pilau here is reminiscent not only of the gold of the ring but the beauty of Rivendell, as captured, likewise, in Tolkien's luminous watercolours of the Hidden Valley.

For a vegan-friendly, health-boosted meal, there's no need to look further than this delicious rice and lentil combination. If you like things a little sweeter, you could stir through a handful of currants or sultanas before serving.

Serves 4
Prep + cook time 40 minutes,
  plus standing

1 tablespoon groundnut oil
1 onion, finely chopped
1 teaspoon ground turmeric
1 tablespoon cumin seeds
1 dried red chilli
1 cinnamon stick
3 cloves
½ teaspoon cardamom seeds, crushed
225 g (7½ oz) basmati rice, rinsed
125 g (4 oz) dried red lentils, rinsed
600 ml (1 pint) vegetable stock
6 tablespoons finely chopped coriander
  leaves
salt

1. Heat the oil in a large saucepan over a medium heat. Add the onion, stir-fry for 6–8 minutes until very soft, then add the spices. Continue to stir-fry for 2–3 minutes until fragrant. Now add the rice and lentils, and stir-fry for a further 2–3 minutes.

2. Add the stock and coriander, season to taste and bring to the boil. Reduce the heat to low, cover the pan and cook gently for 10–12 minutes or until all the liquid has been absorbed. Remove from the heat and allow to stand, covered and undisturbed, for 10–15 minutes. Fluff up the grains with a fork and serve.

Greenwood Pheasant with Blackberries

Here is another dish popular, we think, in the Elvenking's halls, served as a simple supper in the autumn when there are plenty of brambles to be raided along the secret Elven paths that criss-cross Greenwood the Great. While we scarcely come across Elven children in Tolkien's stories, they are nonetheless carefully described in Tolkien's essay 'Of the marriage laws and customs of the Eldar...' They appear, he tells us, much as human children, but much slower to grow and age and long retaining a sense of joy and wonder, 'lingering in the first spring of childhood' and not reaching maturity until 100 years of age. It would be nice to think of blackberrying, then, as the Elven children's business – the pastime of an idyllic and slow-passing youth spent close to nature.

———··———

Meaty game and blackberries have a natural affinity which is why this simple and speedy dish works so well. Serve with the creamy mashed potatoes and steamed kale or cabbage to cut through the sweetness of that heavenly sauce.

Serves 4
Prep + cook time 25 minutes

15 g (½ oz) butter
1 pheasant, divided into 2 legs and
    2 breasts
75 g (3 oz) blackberries
5 tablespoons redcurrant jelly
salt and pepper

1. Heat the butter in a frying pan over a medium heat. Season the pheasant pieces and add to the pan, cooking for 4–5 minutes on each side until golden brown and cooked through. You may need to cook the leg pieces for a little longer. You will know when the meat is done when the juices run clear when you insert a knife into the thickest part of the meat.

2. Add the blackberries and redcurrant jelly and stir until the jelly has melted. Serve immediately with the blackberry sauce spooned over the top.

Nargothrond Chicken

Tolkien's Elves do not only live in forest dwellings and harbour towns, close to the sky, but, like the Dwarves, also in underground cities, delved deep into the sides of hills and river valleys. In this, perhaps, Tolkien was alluding to the Dark Elves of Norse mythology, who dwell deep under the earth. The kindred of Elves known as the Noldor, in particular, are associated with smithery and jewel-making, thus aligning them more closely still with the Dwarves.

We may well wonder what the Elves of this underground realm dined on – no doubt fish from the river Narog, into whose steep banks it is built, together with hunted and gathered foods from the surrounding forests. Perhaps, though, one of the fortress's caves was set aside for raising chickens: here we've imagined a spiced chicken dish served with a bean salad whose bright colours are every bit as bright as Nargothrond's jewels.

This sweet and sticky chicken packs a flavourful punch and is a great midweek meal that uses up the ingredients lurking at the back of your store cupboard.

Serves 4
Prep + cook time 1 hour 10 minutes

8 chicken thighs or drumsticks
1 teaspoon each cumin seeds, fennel
    seeds and dried thyme leaves
¼ teaspoon ground cinnamon
½ teaspoon smoked paprika
1 tablespoon each sunflower oil,
    tomato purée and vinegar
2 tablespoons dark muscovado sugar
2 tablespoons pineapple juice

Bean salad
227 g (7½ oz) can pineapple, juice
    reserved, pineapple chopped
400 g (13 oz) can black-eyed beans
small bunch of coriander, chopped
½ red onion, finely chopped
1 red pepper, cored, deseeded and diced
grated rind and juice of 1 lime

1. Slash the chicken joints 2–3 times with a knife, then place in a roasting tin. Roughly crush the seeds, then mix together with the remaining ingredients and spoon over the chicken.

2. Add 4 tablespoons water to the base of the roasting tin, then place in a preheated oven, 180C (350F), Gas Mark 4, for 40 minutes, spooning the pan juices over occasionally until the chicken is deep brown and the juices run clear when the chicken is pierced with a sharp knife.

3. Meanwhile, make the bean salad. Pour the remaining canned pineapple juice into a bowl and add the chopped pineapple and all the remaining ingredients. Mix together, then serve spoonfuls with the cooked chicken.

Avari Venison Tagine

Tolkien's stories take place largely in the north-west of Middle-earth. While both the Elves and Men originated in the far east of this vast continent, before migrating slowly westward, both the east and the south are only very vaguely described. Indeed, many of Tolkien's toponyms for such regions are simply named after the compass points – Harad means 'South' in Sindarin, and Rhûn, 'East'. They are literally little more than empty white spaces on the map, even though Tolkien implies that they are quite heavily populated, mostly by Men, vassals of Sauron.

And yet there must have been many Avari – the 'unwilling' Elves (page 72) – who lived in the east – a secretive people who lived in the region's vast forests and among its hills and who, though they could never acquire the knowledge and skill of their sundered kinsfolk, the Eldar, nonetheless excelled as singers, hunters, weavers and potters. This might be one of their dishes – brimming with eastern spices and sweet with dried fruits.

The sweetly spiced autumnal dish is a great make-ahead choice. Serve it with your favourite side – couscous, brown rice and quinoa are all good with this – and a dollop of thick yogurt. If you want to ring the changes, replace the venison with shoulder of lamb and reduce the cooking time to 45 minutes.

Serves 4
Prep + cook time 2¼ hours

750 g (1½ lb) venison, cut into cubes

1 onion, chopped

1 garlic clove, crushed

1 teaspoon ground cumin

1 teaspoon ground cinnamon

½ teaspoon ground ginger

1 teaspoon ground turmeric

500 ml (17 fl oz) chicken stock

2 tablespoons tomato purée

1 teaspoon soft dark brown sugar

75 g (3 oz) dried apricots

50 g (2 oz) prunes

50 g (2 oz) flaked almonds, toasted

1. Heat the oil in a large saucepan over a medium heat and brown the meat (you may have to do this in batches), then remove with a slotted spoon and set aside.

2. Add the onion and garlic to the pan and cook for 2–3 minutes, then stir in the spices and cook for a further minute.

3. Return the lamb to the pan with the stock, tomato purée and sugar. Bring to the boil, then simmer with the lid on for 1½ hours. Remove the lid, add the dried fruit and leave to bubble gently for 30 minutes or until the meat is tender.

4. Serve sprinkled with toasted flaked almonds.

Celegorm's Venison Steaks

Tolkien's portrayal of the Elves, in particular of the Noldor, in part draws on the real-world medieval aristocratic elite as shown in epics and romances such as the *Nibelungenlied* or Wolfram von Eschenbach's *Parzifal*. They are first of all warriors but they also engage in pursuits typical of medieval lords and ladies – they feast, they sing, they recite poetry, and, above all, they hunt.

The greatest of the Noldor huntsmen is Celegorm, the third son of Fëanor (page 61), who while in Valinor is a friend of Oromë (page 89), the Huntsman of the Valar (page 66), and receives from him the giant wolfhound Huan as his hunting companion. In Beleriand, with his brother Curufin, he becomes King of Himlad and hunts its forests and moors for deer and wild boar. Perhaps these venison steaks were served in the brothers' feasting hall on their return from the hunt, when songs are sung and music played and Huan sits at his master's feet.

Resting the pepper-and-juniper-crusted venison loin after cooking to allow the juices to creep back in is the key to great results, so resist the urge to cut in right away. Serve the steaks with green beans, redcurrant jelly and chips or boiled potatoes.

Serves 4
Prep + cook time 40–55 minutes

750 g (1½ lb) loin of venison, cut from the haunch
75 g (3 oz) mixed peppercorns, crushed
2 tablespoons juniper berries, crushed
1 egg white, lightly beaten
salt

1. Make sure that the venison fits into your grill pan; if necessary, cut the loin in half to fit.

2. Mix together the peppercorns, juniper berries and some salt in a large, shallow dish. Dip the venison in the egg white, then roll it in the peppercorn mixture, covering it evenly all over.

3. Cook the venison under a preheated hot grill for 4 minutes on each of the 4 sides, turning it carefully so that the crust stays intact. Transfer the loin to a lightly greased roasting tin and cook in a preheated oven, 200°C (400°F), Gas Mark 6, for another 15 minutes for rare and up to 30 minutes for well done (the time will depend on the thickness of the loin of venison).

4. Leave the venison to rest for a few minutes, then slice it thickly and serve.

Oromë's Venison Pie

Of all Tolkien's Valar, Oromë the Huntsman and Lord of Forests is perhaps the closest to the Eldar. It is he who first discovers the Firstborn while hunting the creatures of Morgoth under the stars in the far east of Middle-earth and helps guide them on their Great Journey into the West. In the creation of this Vala, Tolkien was inspired by an amalgam of figures from real-world mythology and folklore: among them, the Norse god Heimdall, who possesses the resounding hunting horn Gjallarhorn just as Oromë has the horn Valaroma, the Greek mythological huntsman Orion, and the supernatural Wild Huntsmen of European folk tales, such as the English Herne, who ride through the night punishing the wicked.

Although Oromë is indefatigable in hunting down the creatures of Morgoth, we can easily imagine him in a gentler guise, settling down to eat with the foot-sore Elves around a campfire. Sometimes, perhaps, he brings them a haunch of venison – this Valar, we're sure, makes a mean venison casserole.

continued overleaf ⇒

Here a hearty winter casserole – made in a slow cooker – is elevated to something special by adding a crispy puff pastry topping. It's delicious served with roasted parsnips and baby carrots. For an easier version, skip the pie topping and serve the venison with mashed or boiled, mint-flecked potatoes instead.

Serves 4–5

Prep + cook time 8½ –10½ hours

25 g (1 oz) butter

1 tablespoon olive oil, plus extra for greasing

750 g (1½ lb) venison, diced

1 onion, chopped

2 tablespoons plain flour

200 ml (7 fl oz) red wine

250 ml (8 fl oz) lamb or beef stock

3 medium raw beetroot, peeled and cut into 1 cm (½ inch) dice

1 tablespoon redcurrant jelly

1 tablespoon tomato purée

10 juniper berries, roughly crushed

3 sprigs of thyme

1 bay leaf

1 sheet, about 200 g (7 oz), ready-rolled puff pastry

beaten egg, for glazing

salt and pepper

1. Preheat the slow cooker on Low if necessary; see the manufacturer's instructions.

2. Heat the butter and oil in a large frying pan, add the venison a few pieces at a time until all the pieces are in the pan, then fry, stirring, until evenly browned. Scoop the venison out of the pan with a slotted spoon and transfer to the slow cooker pot. Add the onion to the pan and fry for 5 minutes until softened.

3. Stir in the flour, then mix in the wine and stock. Add the beetroot, redcurrant jelly and tomato purée, then the juniper, 2 sprigs of the thyme and the bay leaf. Season with salt and pepper and bring to the boil. Pour the sauce over the venison, cover with the lid and cook on low for 8–10 hours or until tender.

4. When you are almost ready to serve, preheat the oven to 220°C (425°F), Gas Mark 7. Unroll the pastry and trim the edges to make an oval similar in size to the slow cooker pot. Transfer to an oiled baking sheet, flute the edges and add leaves cut from the trimmings. Brush with egg, sprinkle with the remaining thyme leaves stripped from the stem and coarse salt and bake for about 20 minutes until well risen and golden.

5. Stir the venison and spoon onto plates. Cut the pastry into wedges and place on top of the venison.

Indis's Carrot & Apple Nut Roast

The Elves, as we know, are far from being vegetarian, let alone vegan, but perhaps a few – those Vanyar or Laiquendi perhaps who are especially devoted to the Vala Yavanna, 'Giver of Fruits', may have adopted a more 'green' diet, cherishing animal life and using only those fruits, nuts and vegetables they could gather in the wild.

We have named this dish for Indis, the niece of Ingwë, the King of the Vanyar and High King of all the Elves. She was briefly unhappily married to the Noldor Finwë, the High King of the Noldor. After her husband's death at the hands of Melkor, she returns to her people in Valinor with one of her daughters. The remainder of her children, including Fingolfin (page 53), take part in the Flight of the Noldor.

Colourful vegetables, sharp apple, crunchy nuts and fragrant herbs wrapped up in layers of crisp filo pastry – this is a vegan delight that will win over even the meat eaters! Serve with green beans and roasted cherry tomatoes.

Serves 4
Prep + cook time 1 hour

3 tablespoons rapeseed oil
1 onion, finely chopped
½ red pepper, finely chopped
1 celery stick, finely chopped
1 carrot, peeled and coarsely grated
75 g (3 oz) chestnut mushrooms, trimmed and finely chopped
1 green apple, cored and grated
1 teaspoon yeast extract
50 g (2 oz) fresh white breadcrumbs
75 g (3 oz) mixed nuts, such as pistachio, blanched almonds and cooked chestnuts, finely chopped
2 tablespoons pine nuts
2 tablespoons chopped flat-leaf parsley
1 tablespoon chopped rosemary
1 tablespoon wholemeal plain flour
8 sheets of filo pastry

1. Heat 1 tablespoon of the oil in a frying pan, add the onion, red pepper and celery and cook over a gentle heat for 5 minutes until softened. Add the carrot and mushrooms and cook for a further 5 minutes until all the vegetables are tender.

2. Remove the pan from the heat and stir in the grated apple, yeast extract, breadcrumbs, nuts, pine nuts, parsley, rosemary and flour. Season with salt and pepper and mix together.

3. Brush one sheet of filo pastry with some of the remaining oil, then place a second on top. Spoon one quarter of the nut mixture on to one end of the filo pastry and roll up, tucking in the ends as you roll to encase the filling. Put seam side down on a baking sheet. Repeat with the remaining pastry and filling to make 4 rolls. Brush the tops with the rest of the oil.

4. Bake the parcels in a preheated oven, 190°C (375°F), Gas Mark 5, for 20 minutes until golden and crisp.

Thranduil's Beef Casserole

The Elves of Greenwood the Great – otherwise known as Mirkwood – seem to have heartier appetites than most of their kindred. In *The Hobbit*, when Bilbo and his companions first come across the Greenwood Elves, they are gathered around a fire, sitting on sawn tree trunks, roasting meat and drinking – rather more like Boy Scouts than we might expect in this remote region of Middle-earth. The Elvenking – who we learn elsewhere is the Sindarin lord Thranduil, father of Legolas – too, seem rather less than ethereal, being very partial to red wine (see page 157). Tolkien seems to be at pains to depict his Elves to be very different, earthier beings from the Victorian conception of fairies that he knew from his childhood.

This recipe brings together beef and wine in a hearty recipe that I like to think would have been very popular in the Elvenking's hall.

Slow cookers are wonderful gadgets – a bit of prep, then in go all the ingredients and you are free to leave the slow cooker bubbling gently away while you get on with your day. All this hearty casserole needs to go alongside is some rice or mashed potato and perhaps some fine green beans.

Serves 4
Prep + cook time 10½–11½ hours

2 tablespoons olive oil
625 g (1¼ lb) stewing beef, trimmed of fat and cubed
100 g (3½ oz) bacon, diced
300 g (10 oz) small shallots
3 garlic cloves, finely chopped
1 tablespoon plain flour
150 ml (¼ pint) red wine
300 ml (½ pint) beef stock
1 tablespoon tomato purée
small bunch of mixed herbs or a dried bouquet garni
salt and pepper
chopped parsley, to garnish

1. Preheat the slow cooker on Low if necessary; see the manufacturer's instructions.

2. Heat the oil in a large frying pan over a high heat. Add the beef, a few pieces at a time, until all the beef is in the pan, and cook for 5 minutes, stirring, until browned. Use a slotted spoon to transfer the beef to the slow cooker pot.

3. Add the bacon and shallots to the frying pan and cook over a medium heat for 2–3 minutes until the bacon is just beginning to brown. Stir in the garlic and flour, then add the wine, stock, tomato purée and herbs. Season to taste and bring to the boil, stirring.

4. Pour the sauce over the beef, cover and cook for 10–11 hours until the beef is tender. Stir and then garnish with chopped parsley.

Salmar's Pork & Mushroom Pasta

Because Tolkien's creation of his legendarium was near lifelong and underwent so many stages of development, his stories of Middle-earth and beyond contain numerous ambiguities, fragments and mysteries that even his indefatigable editor, his son Christopher Tolkien, was unable to resolve.

One such is the figure of Salmar – a Maia who creates his master Ulmo's sea horns – the Ulumúri – out of conch shells. His name appears just once in *The Silmarillion* and then he seems to have been forgotten. Here's a dish, then, using the conch-shaped conchiglie, to celebrate Salmar and all those intriguing shadows and fragments that so enrich our pleasure as we explore Tolkien's world.

Pour yourself a glass of wine and tuck into a bowl of this richly savoury pasta dish topped with plenty of Parmesan. The recipe suggests conchiglie but any hollow shapes, such rigatoni, penne or orecchiette, that will catch the chunky sauce would be fine.

Serves 4
Prep + cook time 40 minutes

2 tablespoons olive oil
1 onion, finely chopped
1 garlic clove, finely chopped
450 g (14½ oz) minced pork
1 tablespoon tomato purée
250 ml (8 fl oz) dry white wine
150 ml (¼ pint) hot chicken stock
150 g (5 oz) mushrooms, trimmed
    and chopped
75 ml (3 fl oz) double cream
400 g (13 oz) conchiglie pasta
25 g (1 oz) Parmesan cheese, grated,
    plus extra to serve
salt and pepper
chopped flat-leaf parsley, to garnish

1. Heat 1 tablespoon of the oil in a large frying pan, add the onion and cook for a couple of minutes until beginning to soften. Add the garlic and pork and cook, breaking up the meat with the back of a spoon, for 5–10 minutes or until the meat is golden.

2. Stir in the tomato purée and cook for a further 1 minute. Pour over the wine and cook until reduced by half, then add the chicken stock and simmer for 10 minutes.

3. Heat the remaining oil in a separate frying pan. Add the mushrooms and cook for 3 minutes or until golden and soft. Add to the pork mixture, then stir in the cream.

4. Meanwhile, cook the pasta in a large saucepan of salted boiling water according to packet instructions until al dente. Drain, reserving a little of the cooking water, and return to the pan. Stir through the sauce and Parmesan, adding a little cooking water to loosen if needed. Season well.

5. Spoon into serving bowls and serve sprinkled with the parsley and extra Parmesan.

Karkapolka Sausages

Tolkien was an indefatigable linguist and philologist – by the time he left school he had learned a plethora of languages, not only the (for his class) conventional Latin, Greek, French, Italian, Spanish and German, but also, among others, Old and Middle English, Gothic, Old Norse, and Medieval Welsh. To these he would add quite a few more through his career as a professor of Anglo-Saxon at Oxford University.

Not content with real-world languages, both living and dead, from early on he also invented his own, most notably Quenya and Sindarin, each of which went through several phases of evolution – like any real language, indeed, but through the wit and imagination of a single mind, gathering rich, fiendishly complex layers of grammar and vocabulary, phonetics and orthography.

So it comes as no surprise to discover that we know two 'Early Quenya' words for 'wild boar' – úro and karkapolka – the latter derived from the Quenya words for 'tusk' and 'pig' and, in Late Quenya, spelled carcapolca. Take your pick when you serve up this dish to your friends and they ask for the name of the recipe.

When you can't face washing a lot of dishes, this one-pot warming casserole is the recipe to go for. Packed with vegetables and lentils, for a delicious and balanced meal, it's a real crowd-pleaser. You could replace the wild boar sausages with venison sausages, if you like.

Serves 4
Prep + cook time 1 hour

8 wild boar sausages, 525 g
  (1 lb 1 oz) in total
2 tablespoons olive oil
1 onion, chopped
150 ml (¼ pint) red wine
600 ml (1 pint) beef stock
2 tablespoons cranberry sauce
1 tablespoon tomato purée
2 bay leaves
300 g (10½ oz) potatoes, cut into
  2.5 cm (1 inch) chunks
2 carrots, cut into 2 cm (¾ inch)
  chunks
250 g (8 oz) tomatoes, roughly
  chopped
250 g (8 oz) red cabbage, finely
  shredded
1 x 400 g (13 oz) can green lentils,
  rinsed and drained
salt and pepper

1. Cook the sausages under a preheated medium grill for 5 minutes, turning until browned but not cooked through.

2. Meanwhile, heat the oil in large flameproof casserole or heavy-bottomed saucepan over a medium heat. Add the onion and cook for 4–5 minutes until just softened. Add the red wine, stock, cranberry sauce, tomato purée and bay leaves, then season to taste and bring to the boil, stirring.

3. Add the potatoes, carrots, tomatoes, red cabbage and sausages. Cover and simmer 30 minutes or until the sausages and potatoes are cooked through. Add the lentils and cook for a further 5 minutes. Serve in shallow bowls.

Rivendell Roast Lamb

Tolkien's conception of the Elves could change according to his dramatic needs or the readership he had in mind. In *The Hobbit* – a novel written for children with elements of adventure, comedy and fairy tale – even the Elves are mined for laughs. Just before Bilbo, Gandalf and the Dwarves reach Elrond's house in Rivendell, they comes across a party of Elves singing and cooking supper out in the open over open fires. Even though the Elves living in the Hidden Valley are largely Noldor and supposedly high-minded, they seem rather frivolous compared to their kindred in *The Lord of the Rings*: their songs are nonsensical and their jibes teasing – even Thorin's venerable beard becomes the object of their fun.

However, for all their merriment, they are hospitable to the new arrivals, even if these are largely made up of Dwarves, inviting them to join them in their al fresco supper. The Dwarves rather roughly decline, wanting to reach Elrond's house where perhaps a better supper is on offer. We might have preferred to stay, however, and sup with the boisterous Elves – especially if this roast lamb was on the menu!

⌐—‥⌐

Roast lamb gets an Italian twist here with rice, succulent semi-dried tomatoes, peppers and plenty of garlic combining for a flavour sensation.

Serves 4
Prep + cook time 1¾ hours

2 red peppers, deseeded and halved
50 g (2 oz) wild rice, cooked
5 garlic cloves, chopped
5 semi-dried tomatoes, chopped
2 tablespoons chopped flat-leaf parsley
625 g (1¼ lb) boneless leg of lamb,
  butterflied
4 artichoke halves
salt and pepper

1. Put the pepper halves in a roasting tin and cook in a preheated oven, 180°C (350°F), Gas Mark 4, for 20 minutes, until the skin has blackened and blistered. Cover with damp kitchen paper and set aside. When the peppers are cool enough to handle, peel off the skin and chop the flesh. (Leave the oven on.)

2. Mix together one of the chopped peppers, the rice, garlic, tomatoes and parsley. Season to taste.

3. Put the lamb on a board and make a horizontal incision, almost all the way along, to make a cavity for stuffing. Fold back the top half, spoon in the stuffing and fold back the top. Secure with skewers.

4. Cook the lamb for 1 hour, basting frequently, and adding the artichokes and other pepper for the last 15 minutes of cooking time. Slice the lamb and serve immediately.

Hunting & Gathering with the Elves

Hunting and gathering was successfully practised by us human beings for millions of years before the development of agriculture. It combined the collection of nuts, fruits, roots, vegetables, eggs and seafood with the scavenging of meat from already-dead animals and also, increasingly, the hunting of live ones. Many early peoples also probably used what is known as forest gardening – the nurturing of existing edible plant species in a woodland and forest setting – to create a kind of natural larder and more dependable food source. Even after the Neolithic or Agricultural Revolution some 11,000 to 12,000 years ago, humans continued to supplement agriculture produce with some hunting and gathering, with hunting increasingly practised by elites alone.

Tolkien's Elves, who begin their existence in the far east of Middle-earth, seem to have begun their existence as hunter-gatherers, collecting fruits and berries from the wooded shores of Cuiviénen, a gulf on the Inland Sea of Helcar, as well as seafood from the waters. Tolkien portrays this era in the existence of the Elves as a kind of lost age of innocence and plenty – the way, indeed, in which the Eldar themselves seem to have perceived it, as expressed in their saying 'And to Cuiviénen there is no returning'. There are no doubt comparisons to be drawn between Cuiviénen and the Garden of Eden, both symbolic of an atavistic nostalgia for a lost original home where nature itself spontaneously provided all wants and needs.

The Elves also probably practised hunting and gathering during the Great Journey into the West. Since they were on the move and ignorant of the landscapes they were passing through, finding enough to eat would have been much more challenging, necessitating the supply of waybread – coimas in Quenya – to the Elves by the Vala Oromë. The Elves who reached Aman were no doubt taught agriculture by the Valar, especially by Yavanna and her followers. Among the Elves who remained in Beleriand, we might conjecture that the Sindar of Doriath practised a kind of forest gardening, as taught to them by the Maia Melian and perhaps by the Ent-wives too, while the Falathrim – the Teleri of Beleriand's coast – no doubt became expert fishermen. It seems likely that, throughout the long ages, the Sindarin Elves of Middle-earth never gave up hunting and gathering and practised agriculture only on the smallest of scales, as witnessed in the growing of corn for coimas/lembas bread in small forest clearings. For the Noldor – who went to Valinor but who returned to Middle-earth as exiles – hunting seems to have become an almost aristocratic pursuit, though there is little indication of social hierarchy among Tolkien's Elves, even if there are clearly leading families and dynasties.

Tolkien tells us little or nothing about how the Elves produce their food in *The Lord of the Rings* – but, in the Elvish meal eaten by the Hobbits at Woody End and subsequent ones in Lothlórien, we get the sense that such food – gained whether by hunting and gathering, forest gardening or small-scale agriculture – always arose out of the Elves' thorough understanding of, and collaboration with, the natural world around them.

Feasting
& Sharing

Feasts and feasting are commonplace among almost all the Peoples of Middle-earth, the Elves included. Unsurprisingly, as in the real-world, feasting and sharing food have been a hallmark of societies for thousands of years. As a renowned Anglo-Saxon scholar, Tolkien knew well how, in Germanic cultures as elsewhere, feasts established or consolidated societal connections and obligations, bringing together host and guest, kin and stranger, even friend and enemy – with the shared meal a symbol of unity and fraternity. In Anglo-Saxon culture the mead-hall where drink and food flowed easily stood at the fulcrum of a flourishing, functioning society.

In Elvish Beleriand, Tolkien constructed a world much like Anglo-Saxon England or Viking Scandinavia, in which a complex network of kings and kingdoms is tied together by kinship and marriage yet threatened by rivalry and enmity. As we see in the Feast of Reuniting (page 120), held by the Noldorin king Fingolfin, feasting is one way in which the Elves smooth over their differences and forged new alliances – even if tensions are never far below the surface.

In this section we've brought together a host of Elvish feasting dishes – from Arwen's Wedding Feast Dish to Egladil Courgette Fritters – to help you woo your friends and family and maybe even an enemy or two! Food is the ultimate conciliator – by sharing food we recognize our common humanity or, in the case of the Eldar, our Elven-kinship. Almien! – Cheers! – as Tolkien fans say.

Valinorian Potatoes

The Hobbit Samwise Gamgee may pine for home-grown 'tatties' freshly dug from the Gaffer's garden at Number 3, Bagshot Row, but we think that Valinor is the real home of the potato. In the real world, as we all know, the wild potato was first domesticated by Native Americans some ten thousand years ago in the region of what is now Peru. By the time of the Inca – in the 14th and 15th centuries – potatoes had become the staple food of the region, stored up through the year either by dehydration or fermentation as tocosh. Today there are thousands of potato varieties in Peru alone, in all sorts of colours and sizes – far beyond the Gaffer's dreams, certainly.

This simple potato sharing dish might well have been served at festivals in Valinor, eaten by Valar and Elves alike as they meet in meadows beneath the walls of the capital city, Valmar, something like the Inca Cusco, a fabled city of golden roofs. Sam, after his journey across the Sundering Seas, will be in for a real treat!

⌐—·⋯—⌐

Hot, crunchy, cheesy potato skins and a creamy, chive-flecked dip – everyone will love this. Serve with pre-dinner drinks and watch it disappear in a flash! If you're pushed for time, then use ready-made tzatziki or salsa for dipping instead.

Serves 6
Prep + cook 15 minutes, plus potato baking

6 large potatoes, baked and left
   to go cold
150 g (5 oz) grated Cheddar cheese
1 tablespoon olive oil

For the soured cream dip
200 g (7 oz) soured cream
1 garlic clove, crushed
1 tablespoon chopped chives
salt and pepper

1. To make the dip, combine the ingredients in a bowl and season to taste.

2. Take the cooled potatoes and cut into quarters. Scoop out and discard the potato flesh (or use for another recipe). Transfer the skins to a bowl, pour over the olive oil and carefully mix with your hands.

3. Place the skins cut-side down on a baking sheet and cook under a preheated hot grills for 2 minutes. Turn the skins over and carefully sprinkle a little cheese on to each skin. Cook for a further 2 minutes until the cheese is melted.

4. Serve immediately with the dip.

Egladil Courgette Fritters

In *The Lord of the Rings*, to bid farewell to the Fellowship, Celeborn and Galadriel hold a feast on the grass at Egladil – the angle of land between the Rivers Anduin and Celebrant. Although it is the only time that the Lord and Lady of Lothlórien eat with their guests during their stay, Tolkien says nothing of the food and drink served, perhaps because Frodo – through whose eyes we largely see the feast – is absorbed by thoughts of the Quest to come and eats and drinks very little. We are free to imagine, then, what dishes are set before the Fellowship …

These courgette fritters are quintessentially Elvish – the very freshest and best produce simply prepared to produce the maximum of flavour. Eat these and imagine the Mallorn trees towering above your head and clusters of golden Elanor flowers at your feet.

Crispy on the outside and creamy inside, these little courgette fritters are the perfect snack for sharing. Serve straight from the pan with the Soured Cream Dip on page 104 or with sweet chilli sauce for dipping. You can add some finely chopped mint or swap out the Parmesan for feta.

Serves 8
Prep + cook time 30 minutes

8 courgettes, trimmed and grated
8 tablespoons self-raising flour
80 g (3 oz) Parmesan cheese, grated
4 tablespoons olive oil

1. Place the grated courgette on a clean tea towel and squeeze out any excess moisture. Place in a bowl with the flour and grated Parmesan and mix together well.

2. Squeeze into walnut-sized balls and then gently flatten.

3. Heat the oil in a deep frying pan and, working in batches, fry the fritters for 2–3 minutes on each side until golden.

Coimas

Coimas is the original Lembas bread – given to the Elves by Oromë for their journey westward across Middle-earth en route to Valinor. This Quenya word means 'life-bread', implying its key role in sustaining and nurturing the Elves during their long trek. The bread was made from the corn (wheat) of Yavanna, so it also seems to have had a sacred quality, too – something akin to the manna provided by God to the Israelites during their 40-year trek through the wilderness on their way to Canaan, the Promised Land.

An irresistible combination of fluffy, chewy bread, oozy melted cheese and a runny baked egg, these meal-in-one breads are a little fiddly to prepare but absolutely worth it.

Serves 3
Prep + cook time 40 minutes, plus proving

For the dough
200 ml (7 fl oz) warm water, plus up to 200 ml (7 fl oz) extra
1 tablespoon quick-acting yeast
1 kg (2 lb 4 oz) plain flour
200 ml (7 fl oz) warm milk
50 ml (2 fl oz) olive oil
1 large egg
1 teaspoon granulated sugar
1 teaspoon fine salt

For the filling
100 g (3½ oz) mozzarella cheese, grated
100 g (3½ oz) feta cheese, crumbled
pinch of cayenne pepper
3 large eggs plus 1 egg, beaten, for brushing

1. In a small bowl, combine the measured warm water with the yeast. In a large bowl, mix together the remaining dough ingredients and add the yeast mixture. Knead by hand or with a dough hook until it forms a smooth, elastic dough. Add up to 200 ml (7 fl oz) extra warm water if needed. Cover with clingfilm and leave to rise in a warm place for 2 hours.

2. To make the filling, combine both cheeses and add a pinch of cayenne pepper.

3. Turn out the dough onto a lightly floured surface. Punch down the dough and divide into 3 pieces. Cover with greased clingfilm and leave to rest for 15 minutes.

4. Roll each piece of pastry into an oval. Spoon one-third of the filling into the centre and spread out, leaving a 2.5 cm (1 inch) margin around the edges. Pull the edges of the pastry around the filling and twist the ends to form a boat shape. Place on a baking tray lined with baking parchment.

5. Brush the pastry with the beaten egg and bake in a preheated oven, 200°C (400°F), Gas Mark 6, for 12–15 minutes. Remove from the oven, make a shallow indentation in the filling of each and crack in an egg. Return to the oven and bake for a further 3–4 minutes or until the eggs are set to your liking.

Starlight Tabbouleh

Tolkien's Elves are closely associated with stars and starlight. The Firstborn first awoke under the stars – before the making of the Sun and the Moon – and lived for many years solely by starlight. When the Vala Oromë first comes across the Elves he calls them the Eldar, meaning 'of the stars'. Even after the Sun and Moon appear in the sky, the Elves retain their love of and affinity with starlight, as we see in the portrayal of the Elf-maid Lúthien, who is first seen by Beren dancing at moonrise in the forest of Doriath, her eyes 'as grey the starlit evening'.

In some ways, in portraying the Elves, at least in their origins, as nocturnal beings, he overturns the usual association of night with evil – here the starlit sky is associated with peace, harmony and closeness to the divine. In this simple dish jewel-like white pomegranate seeds are used to represent the stars above Middle-earth.

Loaded with lovely flavours, this Middle Eastern salad is made with chopped green herbs and bulgar wheat, and is perfect to share at barbecues as a delicious side to grilled chicken, fish and meat. If you can't find white pomegranate seeds, red will do just fine.

Serves 4
Prep + cook time 15 minutes, plus cooling

300 g (10 oz) bulgar wheat
4 tablespoons each chopped coriander, parsley and mint
2 tomatoes, diced
3 tablespoons extra virgin olive oil
3 tablespoons red wine vinegar
100g (3½ oz) white pomegranate seeds
salt and pepper

1. Cook the bulgar wheat according to the packet instructions. Drain well, put into a serving bowl and set aside to cool slightly.

2. Stir in the coriander, mint, parsley, tomatoes, oil, vinegar and season with some salt and pepper. Scatter over the pomegranate seeds and serve.

A Dish for Aragorn & Arwen's Wedding

Packed full of flavour and layering richly savoury and colourful veg, this vegetarian moussaka is topped with a creamy yogurt and feta layer, instead of the more traditional béchamel. Serve it with garlic bread and salad or with wilted kale or spinach.

Serves 4
Prep + cook time 1 hour 10 minutes

5 tablespoons olive oil

1 onion, chopped

2 garlic cloves, finely chopped

500 g (1 lb) courgettes, cut into chunks

250 g (8 oz) closed cup mushrooms, quartered

1 red pepper, cored, deseeded and cut into chunks

1 orange pepper, cored, deseeded and cut into chunks

2 x 400 g (13 oz) cans chopped tomatoes

2 rosemary stems, leaves stripped from stems

½ tablespoon finely chopped thyme leaves

1 teaspoon caster sugar

2 aubergines, sliced

3 eggs

300 g (10 oz) Greek-style yogurt

large pink of grated nutmeg

75 g (3 oz) feta cheese, grated

salt and pepper

1. Heat 1 tablespoon of the oil in a frying pan, add the onion and fry for 5 minutes, stirring, until just beginning to go brown. Add the garlic, courgettes, mushrooms and peppers and fry for 2–3 minutes.

2. Stir in the tomatoes, rosemary, thyme, sugar and season with salt and pepper. Bring to the boil, then cover and simmer for 15 minutes. Tip into a shallow ovenproof dish, leaving enough space to add the aubergines and topping.

3. Meanwhile, heat 2 tablespoons of the oil in a clean frying pan and fry half the aubergine slices until softened and golden on both sides. Arrange, overlapping, on top of the tomato mixture. Repeat with the remaining aubergine slices and oil.

4. Stir the eggs, yogurt, nutmeg and a little pepper together in a bowl, then pour over the aubergines. Sprinkle with the feta and bake in preheated oven, 180°C (350°F), Gas Mark 4, for 30–35 minutes until piping hot.

Tolkien is primarily a writer of epic and myth – the world of *The Hobbit*, *The Lord of the Rings* and even *The Silmarillion* is largely oriented towards male friendship and masculine military virtues such as bravery and loyalty. However, there are also powerful elements of romance – in the love stories of, among others, Beren and Lúthien, Eärendil and Elwing, Faramir and Éowyn, and Aragorn and Arwen – not forgetting, of course, that of Sam Gamgee and the farmer's daughter Rosie Cotton. In some ways, *The Lord of the Rings* ends like a Victorian novel, with a flurry of weddings signalling the restoration of peace and order after a period of strife and uncertainty.

The marriage of the Dúnedain king Aragorn and the Half-elven princess Arwen on Midsummer's Day TA 3019, has an especially symbolic role in this respect: after the end of the War of the Ring, their wedding ushers in a new age, reconciling the lands and peoples of western Middle-earth. In one sense, their union redeems that of their mutual ancestors Beren and Lúthien, which ended tragically and is part of the events that lead to the catastrophic close of the First Age.

This crowd-pleasing dish could well have been served at Arwen's wedding banquet in the halls of Minas Tirith, bringing together, as it does, some of Gondor's finest, Mediterranean-like produce – vibrant vegetables and strong-flavoured herbs. See in a bright new age and celebrate the nuptials of the king and queen of the Reunited Kingdom.

Mereth Aderthad Paella

Here is another celebration dish whose vibrant colours and intense flavours will bring your hurrying guests to the table. We have named it for the Mereth Aderthad, the Feast of Reuniting, held by Fingolfin, the King of the Noldor, soon after the beginning of the First Age. All the Elves of Beleriand, both Noldor and Sindar, attend, and the harmony and friendship that prevail there seems to herald a period of peace and goodwill, free from the threat of the Dark Lord, Morgoth. As we know, things do not turn out quite as planned. Such feasts of apparent unity but hidden rivalries abound in myth and epic, of course – from the *Nibelungenlied* to Arthurian romance – but perhaps this dish will make sure that, at your feast at least, all things go smoothly.

A vegetarian take on the classic Spanish paella, this is a great meal to share with friends. Pile it up on a large platter, place it in the centre of the table, add a big green salad and let everyone dig in.

Serves 4
Prep + cook time 45 minutes

4 tablespoons olive oil
1 onion, chopped
pinch of saffron threads
225 g (7½ oz) arborio rice
1.2 litres (2 pints) vegetable stock
175 g (6 oz) fine asparagus spears,
    trimmed and cut into 5 cm (2 inch)
    lengths
bunch of spring onions, cut into strips
175 g (6 oz) midi plum tomatoes on
    the vine, halved
125 g (4 oz) frozen peas
3 tablespoons flaked almonds, toasted
3 tablespoons chopped flat-leaf parsley
salt

1. Heat 1 tablespoon of the oil in a large, heavy-based frying pan, add the onion and saffron and cook over a medium heat, stirring frequently, for 5 minutes, until the onion is softened and golden. Add the rice and stir well, then season with some salt. Add the stock and bring to the boil, then cover and simmer, stirring occasionally, for 20 minutes until the stock is almost all absorbed and the rice is tender and cooked through.

2. Meanwhile, heat the remaining oil in a separate frying pan, add the asparagus and spring onions and cook over a medium heat for 5 minutes until softened and lightly charred in places. Remove from the pan with a slotted spoon. Add the vine tomatoes to the pan and cook for 2–3 minutes on each side until softened.

3. Add the peas to the rice and cook for a further 2 minutes, then add the asparagus, spring onions and tomatoes and gently toss through. Scatter with the almonds and parsley and serve.

Food for the Great Journey: Outdoor Cooking

Tolkien's Elves have many homes and homelands but they are above all migrants, travellers and wanderers. When we first encounter a party of Elves in *The Lord of the Rings* they are journeying through the quieter, wooded places of The Shire, camping, cooking and eating out in the wild.

The story of the Elves begins, indeed, with the Great Journey, when, at the bequest of the Valar, the majority of the Firstborn make their trek from the far east of Middle-earth towards the far west in the days when the Sun and the Moon had not yet risen. It's a journey that is echoed through the aeons of Elvish history – in the Flight of the Noldor across the Helcaraxë (page 53) and the diaspora of the Eldar during the Wars of Beleriand.

Tolkien tells us that the Valar helped sustain the Elves during their journey with coimas bread (page 108) made from the corn of Yavanna – the prototype of the Lembas made by the Elves ever after. No doubt, the Elves supplemented this with other hunted and foraged foods, too, however – so here we have commemorated the Great Journey with a selection of dishes which, while you will likely make them on the barbecue in your own backyard, will evoke something of the adventure of the Elves' starlit march.

Ꝛ

Summer means barbecues: warm days, light-filled evenings, friends, laughter and great food cooked on the fire. These recipes will get your barbecue off to a sizzling start. With a choice of spicy chicken or minted lamb kebabs, lemony mackerel and a medley of vegetables transformed into colourful skewers, plus herby tabbouleh to serve on the side, there's something to please everyone. Just add icy-cold drinks!

Nandor Barbecued Chicken

In *The Silmarillion* and elsewhere Tolkien describes how some of the Elves who took part in the Great Journey turned aside from their path – sometimes out of fear of the awe-inspiring natural features they came across, such as the Misty Mountains, sometimes out of wonder at the beauty of Middle-earth. Among the Elves who abandoned the march were some of the Teleri who, led by Lenwë, went southward on reaching the Great River, settling in the woodlands in the Vales of Anduin. They became known as the Nandor – 'Those who go back' – some of whom would later settle in Lothlórien.

Perhaps it was at this early stage that the Nandor started to build treehouses – primitive versions of the tree-mansions of Lothlórien. They were adept woodcrafters and skilled with bow and arrow. Here we have imagined a dish perfect for a woodland supper, using meat shot during the day's hunting. Chicken is used in this recipe, but for a more authentic touch you could use pheasant breast.

The fragrant smoke is drifting up slowly to the treetops where it mingles with the stars … Perhaps, given the fate of so many of the Elves who reached Beleriand and beyond, the Nandor didn't make such a bad choice, after all.

Serves 6
**Prep + cook time 20 minutes,
  plus marinating**

500 g (1 lb) skinless chicken thigh
  fillets, cut into thin strips
2 garlic cloves, crushed
2 teaspoons peeled and grated fresh
  root ginger
1 red bird's eye chilli, deseeded and
  finely chopped
grated rind of 1 lime
2 tablespoons light soy sauce
1 tablespoon sesame oil
1 teaspoon caster sugar
¼ teaspoon black pepper
6 large lemon grass stalks

1. Place the chicken thighs in a shallow non-metallic dish. Combine all the remaining ingredients except for the lemon grass stalks and leave to marinate for 1 hour.

2. Peel and discard a few of the outer layers of the lemon grass stalks so that they are a little finer. Cut the thinner end into a point and thread the marinated chicken on to each stalk at this end, zig-zagging backwards and forwards as you go. Cook on a hot barbecue or under a preheated hot grill for 3–4 minutes on each side, brushing with the marinade halfway through. Serve hot.

Belegaer Barbecued Mackerel

Tolkien tells us how the Teleri arrived too late on the shores of Belegaer to be ferried across the Great Sea and so had to wait for Ulmo's return with the island-raft Tol Eressëa (page 45). Befriended by the Maia Ossë, they fell in love with the sea and so became known as the Sea-elves. Perhaps the sea reminded them of the Inland Sea of Helcar where the Elves had first awakened.

It is not hard to imagine the Teleri sitting round campfires on the beach as they waited under the starlight and with the sound of the waves all around them. They were famous singers, too – so their voices would have melded with the rush and roar of the sea. From time to time they would have caught fish and roasted them simply over their fires. No wonder, then, that – when Ulmo finally returned – a large number chose to stay in Middle-earth.

Serves 4
Prep + cook time 20 minutes

4 mackerel, about 400 g (13 oz) each
olive oil, for brushing
3 lemons, thinly sliced, plus
2 tablespoons lemon juice
salt and pepper

1. Slash each mackerel 3—4 times on each side with a sharp knife. Brush with a little oil and season inside and out with salt and pepper. Using cooking string, tie 3 lemon slices on each side of the fish. Brush the lemon with a little oil and cook the mackerel on a hot barbecue or under a preheated hot grill for 4—5 minutes on each side until lightly charred and cooked through. Set aside to rest for 5 minutes before serving.

Vanyarin Barbecue Lamb

The fair-headed kindred of Elves known as the Vanyar are easily forgotten as we, Tolkien's readers, become embroiled in the tales of the Noldor and the Teleri and the Wars of Beleriand. Of all the Elves, however, they come closest to completing the Great Journey in its fullest sense: not content with reaching the shores of Aman, they eventually move to the Valinorian capital, Valmar, to live alongside the Valar, in the full light of the Two Trees.

We learn very little of the Vanyar, except for a few of their names, but of all the Elves they live the most settled and peaceful lives. For all their beauty and nobility, perhaps, too, they also live the simplest lives, farming the rich soils of Valinor and raising sheep and cattle. When their work was done, perhaps they ate supper out in the open air, roasting meats in their meadows, drinking the mead-like miruvórë and reciting their exquisite poetry.

Serves 4
Prep + cook time 15 minutes,
  plus chilling

500 g (1 lb) boneless leg of lamb,
  minced
1 small onion, finely chopped
1 garlic clove, crushed
1 tablespoon chopped rosemary
6 anchovies in oil, drained and
  chopped
olive oil, for brushing
salt and pepper

1. Combine the lamb, onion, garlic, rosemary, anchovies and some salt and pepper in a bowl and use your hands to work them together. Divide into 12 and shape into even-sized, sausage-shaped patties. Chill for 30 minutes.

2. Thread the patties on to metal skewers, brush lightly with oil and cook on a barbecue or under a preheated hot grill for 3—4 minutes on each side until cooked through. Serve hot.

Blue Mountains Vegetable Skewers

E red Luin – or the Blue Mountains – was the second great chain of mountains that the Elves had to negotiate to reach the shores of the Belegaer, the great western ocean. Beyond the mountains lay Beleriand, which at this time lay empty under the starlight. The Blue Mountains were less mighty than the Misty Mountains, but were still a daunting prospect.

We can well imagine how at this point supplies might have been running low, even of the wonderful coimas (page 108). To supplement their diet the Elves may well have foraged for wild vegetables and herbs in the upland forests and meadows of the mountains, roasting them over their fires after their day's trek. The heady fragrance of the rosemary would have raised their spirits – their long march would soon be over.

Serves 4
Prep + cook time 30 minutes, plus marinating

3 tablespoons olive oil

1 tablespoon chopped rosemary

2 courgettes, thickly sliced

1 large red pepper, deseeded and quartered

16 button mushrooms, trimmed

16 large cherry tomatoes

salt and pepper

ready-made tzatziki, to serve

1. In a large bowl combine the oil with the rosemary and some salt and pepper. Add the courgette, pepper, mushrooms and cherry tomatoes to the oil, toss well and marinate for 15 minutes.

2. Thread the vegetables on to metal skewers, alternating the vegetables so all the skewers have a good variety.

3. Cook the skewers on a hot barbecue or under a preheated hot grill for 10—15 minutes, turning halfway through, until all the vegetables are cooked. Serve hot with tzatziki.

The Great Feast & the Heroic Age of the Elves

Feasts are characteristic of epic literature, found in works from *The Odyssey* of the ancient Greeks and the *Mahābhārata* of ancient India to the *Kalevala* of the Finnish and 'Beowulf' of the Anglo-Saxons, so it is unsurprising to find them mentioned frequently in *The Silmarillion*, the collection of tales depicting Middle-earth's heroic First Age. There, as elsewhere, feasts are held for various reasons – celebratory, religious and reconciliatory. The Valar, we are told, hold a feast to celebrate the end of their labours in forming Arda and another 'high feast' in praise of Eru, the One (the supreme deity). Among the Elves, Fëanor appears at feasts in the Noldor city of Tirion in Aman wearing the Silmarils proudly displayed on his brow, and Fingolfin holds a 'great feast' – known as the Mereth Aderthad (the Feast of Reuniting) – to bring together the Elves of Beleriand in a time of peace and prosperity. Such feasts are often joyous, Tolkien tells us, marked by much music-making and singing and no doubt dancing, too, but, sadly, he tells us next to nothing about the food or drink consumed, with the exception of the mead-like cordial miruvórë. Largely, we must imagine these things for ourselves.

Feasts are also a feature of *The Hobbit* and *The Lord of the Rings*, even if it is the intimate meals – the breakfast and the supper – that we remember best. *The Hobbit* begins with an impromptu 'feast' of the most basic, greedy kind as Thorin and his companions dig into the contents of Bilbo's beloved pantries. The feast proper remains mostly closely associated with the Elves, however – in the halls of Rivendell and the Elvenking. At the beginning of *The Lord of the Rings* the feast is likewise to some extent 'domesticated' as the 'party' – the 'pleasant Feast' celebrating Bilbo's 111st and Frodo's 33rd birthdays and the 'Hundredweight Feast' of the following year held in Bilbo's honour in his absence – and it only as the narrative itself tips over entirely into the heroic mode, beginning when the Hobbits reach Elvish Rivendell, that 'great feasting' makes its appearance, with a feast to celebrate the victory at the Ford of Bruinen.

Thereafter there is a feast at the departure from Elvish Lothlórien, after which all feasting is at an end until the 'eucatastrophe' of the book's first ending and the midsummer wedding of Arwen and Aragorn. With this celebration – marking the end of the dominion of the Elves and restoration of the dominion of Men – the association of Elves with the 'great feast' comes to an end, though no doubt there are feasts of joy to come in Valinor as the Elves are welcomed to their final homecoming.

Desserts & Sweet Things

Do the Elves have a sweet tooth? From the contents of Bilbo's larder, with its copious supply of tarts and cakes, we know that Hobbits do, and from the greed of the Thorin and Company when they come to sup with Bilbo so unexpectedly at the beginning of *The Hobbit*, we know that Dwarves do, too. On Men's liking for sweet things we hardly need to pass comment – given their real-world peers. But Elves? Can we really imagine the high-minded Elves, with their taste for poetry and flowers and combating evil, tucking into anything so frivolous as a lemon meringue pie, a sherry-spiked trifle, or a syrup pudding swimming in custard?

Perhaps not ... but a fondness for natural sweetness is certainly not beyond the Elvish palette. Quenya has a word for 'sweet to the taste' – lissë – which seems to refer primarily to the sweetness of honey (the Sindarin equivalent is leich). It is used in Galadriel's Lament to describe the mead of the lofty halls of the Valar, and the Elvish drink miruvor (see pages 148–149), too, is described as having a mead-like sweetness. No doubt lissë/leich would also be applied, too, to the sweetness of berries and orchard fruits – which the Elves also seem to savour, if Gildor's impromptu meal enjoyed by Frodo, Pippin and Sam is anything to go by.

It is honey and fruits, then, that predominate in the following recipes, from Legolas's Bramble Pudding through Hithlum Tart to Yavanna's Fruit Salad. One can be high-minded and indulge oneself from time to time.

Melian's Plum-Topped Cheesecake

We have named this rather sumptuous, alluring cheesecake after the Maia Melian, who in *The Silmarillion* meets and enchants – in both the literal and metaphorical sense – the Telerin Elf Elwë (Thingol) in the nightingale-haunted woods of Nan Elmoth in Beleriand, causing him to forget his people and his journey to Valinor.

In Valinor, Melian has served the two Valar queens Vána and Estë and in the Gardens of Lórien tended to its many fruit trees. With her dark hair and garments of deep red, she is one of Tolkien's most seductive and sensual characters. As a woodland-dwelling enchantress, she has much in common with the feys of Arthurian legend, most notably Vivienne or Nimuë, who ensorcells the wizard Merlin in the forest of Broceliande.

Plums, then, are a fitting fruit for this enticing, tree-loving enchantress. Taste this fabulous cheesecake and you may well understand why Thingol forgets every thought of his kinsfolk and Valinor. How could they possibly compete?

This creamy baked cheesecake, topped with aromatic poached plums, is sure to be popular with friends and family. Any leftover cheesecake will keep for a few days in the fridge and any spare poached plums can be spooned over porridge or atop yogurt for breakfast.

Serves 6
Prep + cook time 1 hour, plus cooling and chilling

480 g (17 oz) ricotta cheese

425 g (15 oz) cream cheese

2 eggs

1 teaspoon vanilla extract

125 g (4 oz) caster sugar

½ small orange

1 teaspoon whole cloves

2 tablespoons dark brown sugar

1 cinnamon stick

175 ml (6 fl oz) water

375 g (12 oz) red plums, halved and pitted

2 tablespoons redcurrant jelly

1. Grease a 500 g (1 lb) loaf tin lightly and line the base and sides with non-stick baking paper. Blend the ricotta and cream cheese with the eggs, vanilla extract and caster sugar until smooth. Turn the mixture into the loaf tin and place in a small roasting tin. Pour hot water into the tin to a depth of 2.5 cm (1 inch) and bake in a preheated oven, 160°C (325°F), Gas Mark 3, for about 40 minutes or until lightly set. Lift the loaf tin out of the water and allow to cool in the tin.

2. Meanwhile, stud the orange with the cloves and place in a heavy-bottomed pan with the brown sugar, cinnamon and measured water. Bring the water to the boil, reduce the heat and add the plums. Cover and cook gently for 5 minutes or until just tender.

3. Lift out the plums and add the redcurrant jelly to the pan. Boil the liquid for about 2 minutes until reduced and syrupy. Remove the orange and cinnamon stick and pour the syrup over the plums. Let the syrup cool, then chill until ready to serve.

4. Remove the cheesecake from the tin, peel off the paper and cut into slices. Serve topped with the poached plums.

Dorthonion Heather Honey Sponge

Tolkien mentions honey regularly in his works. Beekeeping appears to be practised by most of the peoples of Middle-earth, with honey used to sweeten cakes and other foodstuffs and, of course, to make mead. The best-known beekeeper, of course, is the Skin-changer Beorn in *The Hobbit* who is a dab hand at making honey cakes.

We may conjecture, however, that beekeeping was originally an Elvish activity, which was perhaps taught to them by the Valar in Valinor. In *The Lord of the Rings*, Galadriel sings a lament for the Elves in exile, mourning the memory of the 'sweet mead in lofty halls beyond the West' and the emptiness of her cup in Middle-earth. There is a recording of Tolkien giving a fine rendition of Galadriel's Lament – in the original Quenya, of course.

For this pudding we have specified heather honey, perhaps like that made in Dorthonion, in the north of Beleriand, whose characteristic landscapes were forest and heather-covered heathlands. For some time this was the kingdom of the Noldorin Elves Angrod and Aegnor, until it was overrun by Morgoth after the Dagor Bragollach – the Battle of the Sudden Flame.

⌐—··—⌐

A great one for lunchboxes, this cake is beautifully sweet because of the honey. You can ring the changes by adding a teaspoon of mixed spice or ground cinnamon to the mix and it also works really well with pears instead of the apples.

Makes a 1 kg (2 lb) loaf cake
Prep + cook time 1¼ hours

125 g (4 oz) plain flour

50 g (2 oz) wholemeal flour

1 teaspoon baking powder

3 tablespoons golden caster sugar

125 g (4 oz) heather honey, plus extra
   to serve

125 g (4 oz) butter, softened

3 eggs, lightly beaten

1 teaspoon vanilla extract

50 ml (2 fl oz) apple juice

1 large dessert apple, peeled, cored
   and chopped

1. Line a 1 kg (2 lb) loaf tin with non-stick baking paper. Sift the flours and baking powder into a large bowl. Mix in the sugar, honey, butter, eggs, vanilla extract and apple juice. Stir through the apple.

2. Spoon the mixture into the prepared tin and bake in a preheated oven, 180°C (350°F), Gas Mark 4, for 1 hour. To see if it is cooked, insert a skewer in the centre of the loaf – if it comes out clean it is done, but if cake mix is attached to the skewer it will need another 10 minutes.

3. Remove the cake from the oven and turn out on to a wire rack. Peel off the baking paper and leave to cool. Serve cut into slices with a drizzle of honey.

Galadriel's Cookies

Galdariel and cookies ... unimaginable! But think again: Galadriel is, as Frodo witnesses, not only the majestic queen, Noldorin exile, possessor of the Elven ring Vilya (page 83), and survivor of thousands of years of Elven history, but also wife, mother and friend, the thoughtful, tender Elf-lady who bestows gifts of both power and simplicity on the Fellowship at their parting – from the Elfstone for Aragorn to a single silver nut of a Mallorn tree for Sam. How touching is that grey wooden box marked with a 'G' that she hands to the awestruck Hobbit?

Here's a simple almond biscuit, then, made by Galadriel when she feels like being just a normal Elf-maid, to share with her attendants on a lazy day under the Mallorn trees.

When friends come round for coffee, serve up a plate of these crumbly, orange-scented cookies, fresh from the oven. If you swap the plain flour for rice flour and use gluten-free baking powder, then any gluten-intolerant people can safely enjoy them too.

Makes 20
Prep + cook time 20 minutes, plus chilling

75 g (3 oz) polenta

25 g (1 oz) plain flour, plus extra for dusting

25 g (1 oz) ground almonds

½ teaspoon baking powder

75 g (3 oz) icing sugar

50 g (2 oz) butter, cubed

1 egg yolk, beaten

grated rind of 1 orange

25 g (1 oz) flaked almonds

1. Line 2 baking sheets with non-stick baking paper.

2. Place the polenta, flour, ground almonds, baking powder, icing sugar and butter in a food processor and whizz until the mixture resembles fine breadcrumbs. Alternatively, mix together the polenta, flour, ground almonds, baking powder and icing sugar in a large bowl, then add the butter and rub in with the fingertips until the mixture resembles fine breadcrumbs.

3. Add the beaten egg yolk and orange rind and combine to form a firm dough. Wrap in clingfilm and chill in the fridge for 30 minutes.

4. Turn the dough out onto a lightly dusted work surface, roll out thinly and use a 4cm (1½ inch) cutter to cut out 20 cookies, rerolling the trimmings as necessary. Transfer to the prepared baking sheets and sprinkle with the flaked almonds.

5. Bake in a preheated oven, 180°C (350°F), Gas Mark 4, for about 8 minutes until golden. Remove from the oven, leave for a few minutes to harden on the baking sheets, then transfer to a wire rack to cool further.

Teiglin Hazelnut & Pear Cake

Hazels appear quite frequently in Tolkien's writings, often come across by wanderers, questers and exiles as they scramble through Middle-earth's wild, rugged landscapes. Hazels are known for their soft, downy leaves, pale-golden catkins and their winter nuts, sometimes known as cobnuts or filberts, according to the species. No doubt such nuts would have been gathered and eaten by every people of Middle-earth, especially when other foodstuffs scarce. In the real world, protein-rich hazelnuts are often ground up into a meal to add to flour.

There are brakes of hazel growing close to the River Teiglin in Beleriand. It is close to a hazel tree that Tolkien's tragic hero Turin kills the captain of a group of outlaws, Forweg, and then assumes the leadership himself.

Roulades look tricky but are surprisingly easy and very satisfying to make – the trick is to use the baking paper to help you roll it. This dinner-party dazzler combines a nutty, light-as-air sponge with juicy apricots and rich mascarpone.

Serves 6–8
Prep + cook time 50 minutes,
plus cooling

125 g (4 oz) roasted hazelnuts
5 eggs, separated
175 g (6 oz) caster sugar, plus extra
    for sprinkling
1 just-ripe pear, peeled and coarsely
    grated
200 g (7 oz) mascarpone cheese
2 tablespoons icing sugar
250 g (8 oz) fresh apricots, roughly
    chopped

1. Grease and line a 30 x 23 cm (12 x 9 inch) roasting tin with non-stick baking paper. Roughly chop 2 tablespoons of the hazelnuts and reserve, then finely chop the remainder.

2. Whisk the egg yolks and sugar until they are thick and pale and the whisk leaves a trail. Fold in the finely chopped hazelnuts and the pear. Whisk the whites into stiff, moist-looking peaks. Fold a large spoonful into the nut mix to loosen it, then gently fold in the remaining egg whites.

3. Spoon the mixture into the prepared tin. Bake in a preheated oven, 180°C (350°F), Gas Mark 4, for 15 minutes until golden brown and the top feels spongy. Cover and leave to cool for at least 1 hour.

4. Beat the mascarpone and icing sugar until soft. On a work surface, cover a damp tea towel with baking paper and sprinkle with sugar. Turn the roulade on to the paper and remove the tin and paper.

5. Spread the roulade with the mascarpone mixture, then with the apricots. Roll up the roulade, starting from the short end nearest you, using the paper and tea towel to help. Transfer the roulade to a serving plate, join side down, sprinkle over the reserved hazelnuts and cut into thick slices.

Goldberry's Honeycomb Stack

Tolkien fans debate long and hard over the mysterious nature and origin of Tom Bombadil and his wife, Goldberry – kindly, hospitable beings whom Frodo and his companions encounter soon after their departure from the Shire. All we are told is that he is known to the Elves as the 'oldest and fatherless' and that she is 'daughter of the river' – leaving us to conjecture whether both are nature spirits, perhaps Maiar in the service of Yavanna (see page 7) and Ulmo (see page 50), respectively. Others have suggested that Goldberry is 'only' the daughter of a Maia, and we might even hazard that her father was an Elf – just as Lúthien is the daughter of the Maia Melian and the Sindarin Elf Thingol. Indeed, Goldberry is explicitly compared to 'a young elf-queen', wreathed in flowers just like Lúthien.

Whatever her origin, Goldberry, is closely associated with the bounty of nature. In inviting the Hobbits to stay in the couple's home, Tom conjures up a vision of their household, where Goldberry's table is already laden with, among other delectables, honeycomb and cream, and where roses peep over the window sills.

These delicious double-decker pancakes are a doddle to make: simply assemble and griddle. Or, for an al fresco treat, you can cook them on the barbecue. Serve topped with blueberries, strawberries or raspberries.

Serves 2
Prep + cook time 10 minutes

60 ml (2½ fl oz) double cream, plus extra to serve
30 g (1½ oz) honeycomb or old-fashioned cinder toffee, crumbled
1 teaspoon finely grated lemon rind
65 g (2½ oz) candied lemon peel, finely chopped (optional)
150 ml (¼ pint) lemon curd
6 ready-made Scotch pancakes

1. Put the cream, honeycomb or cinder toffee, lemon rind, candied peel, if using, and lemon curd in a bowl and mix well. Place a dollop of the lemon cream on a pancake, top with a second pancake and another dollop of lemon cream on top, then finish with a third pancake. Repeat the process so that you have two triple-decker lemon pancakes.

2. Cook the pancake stacks on a preheated griddle over medium-high heat for 1–2 minutes, then carefully flip over and cook for a further 1–2 minutes until the outside pancakes are toasted and the lemon cream is beginning to ooze from the sides. Serve immediately.

Vána's Apple Pie

Many of Tolkien's Powers of Arda – his 'gods' and 'goddesses' – can be related to figures in real-world mythologies. This is certainly the case with the beautiful Vána, the younger sister of Yavanna (see page 29), at whose passing flowers spring to life and birds begin to sing. She is clearly related to figures such as the Greek goddesses Persephone – goddess of spring growth – and Hebe – goddess of youth.

Perhaps the closest analogy – one that the Anglo-Saxon specialist Tolkien might have preferred – is with the Norse goddess Iðunn, whose very name may mean 'Ever-young', a epithet likewise of Vána. Iðunn is best known as the keeper of the apples of youth, which keep the gods young, and Vána, too, dwells in gardens of golden flowers and trees, including, no doubt, fruit trees. This golden dessert is for her, then: imagine the immortal Elves dining al fresco in their own orchards and tucking into this divine confection.

❧ ––– ⋯ ––– ❧

Sweet, spiced apples combine with flaky puff pastry in this version of the traditional family favourite. Serve it warm with spoonfuls of crème fraîche or extra-thick cream, or a scoop of the Simbelmynë Ice Cream on page 143.

Serves 6
Prep + cook time 45 minutes

1 kg (2 lb) or about 5 cooking apples, quartered, cored, peeled and thickly sliced

100 g (3½ oz) caster sugar, plus extra for sprinkling

grated rind of 1 small orange

½ teaspoon ground mixed spice or ground cinnamon

3 whole cloves

400 g (13 oz) chilled ready-made puff pastry

a little flour, for dusting

1 egg, beaten

1. Fill a 1.2 litre (2 pint) pie dish with the apples. Mix the sugar with the orange rind, mixed spice and cloves, then sprinkle over the apples.

2. Roll the pastry out on a lightly floured surface until a little larger than the top of the dish. Cut 2 long strips from the edges, about 1 cm (½ inch) wide. Brush the dish rim with a little beaten egg, press the strips on top, then brush these with egg. Lift the remaining pastry over the dish and press the edges together well.

3. Trim off the excess pastry, make small, horizontal cuts around the pastry rim with a small knife (this helps encourage the layers in the pastry to separate and rise), then press the edges of the pie together neatly. Reroll the trimmings and cut out small heart shapes or circles with a small biscuit cutter. Brush the top of the pie with beaten egg, add pastry shapes, then brush these with egg. Sprinkle with a little extra sugar.

4. Bake in a preheated oven, 200°C (400°F), Gas Mark 6, for 20–25 minutes until the pastry is well risen and golden.

Hithlum Tart

Here is another Elvish tart, this one using a mixture of honey and pine nuts. Pines are mentioned in Tolkien's works more than any other tree and are characteristic of many highland landscapes across Middle-earth. In the First Age, the cold, misty region of Hithlum, to the north-west of Beleriand, was near-surrounded by pine-clad mountains, and they also grew in the vicinity of Rivendell, in the lee of the Misty Mountains, their sweet, resinous smell making Bilbo drowsy as he and the Dwarves draw close to Elrond's home.

The Elves no doubt put every one of Yavanna's gifts to good use, the edible seeds of pine trees – rich in protein and carbohydrates – included. Here they are teamed with a flowery honey, to make a filling, tasty tart that would have helped keep out the chill of even the coldest day in Hithlum.

This unusual tart is a delicately balanced combination of sweet honey and crunchy pine nuts. Serve with ice cream, cream or a blob of crème fraîche and drizzled with a little extra honey for a cheffy flourish.

Serves 8–10

Prep + cook time 1 hour 20 minutes

400 g (13 oz) chilled ready-made or homemade sweet shortcrust pastry
100 g (3½ oz) unsalted butter
100g (3½ oz) caster sugar
3 eggs
175 g (6 oz) flower honey, warmed
grated rind and juice of 1 lemon
200 g (7 oz) pine nuts

1. Roll out the pastry thinly on a lightly floured surface and line a 23 cm (9 inch) loose-bottomed baking tin. Prick the base, line with non-stick baking paper, add baking beans and bake blind in a preheated oven, 190°C (375°F), Gas Mark 5, for 15 minutes. Remove the paper and beans and bake for 5 minutes more. Reduce the oven temperature to 180°C (350°F), Gas Mark 4.

2. Cream together the butter with the caster sugar. Beat in the eggs, one at a time, then mix in the warmed honey, the lemon rind and juice and the pine nuts. Pour into the tart case and bake for about 40 minutes until browned and set.

3. Let the tart cool for 10 minutes before serving.

Lemon Meringue & Sea Buckthorn Pie

One of the most glorious sights on Europe's temperate sandy coasts are the banks of sea buckthorn (*Hippophae rhamnoides*), with its clouds of deep-orange berries set amid dark-green spiny leaves. As a scholar of Old English, Tolkien might have especially appreciated this coastal shrub, which the Anglo-Saxons believed, like hawthorn, to ward off harm and was used on magic charms. The Old English rune ðorn (thorn) – was thought to have defensive powers.

We might imagine sea buckthorn growing in the sandy dunes on Middle-earth's north-west coasts, including in First Age Beleriand, in the region known as Falas (Sindarin for 'coast'). The Falathrim – the 'Coast-elves' – were doubtless expert foragers and made good use of this tart berry which tastes something like a mixture of orange and mango.

The sublime blend of creamy lemon filling topped with billowy sweet meringue makes this classic pie such a winner. And it is even better served with wonderfully colourful sea buckthorn sauce. Picked fresh, sea buckthorn berries taste very tart, but cook them with a little sugar or maple syrup to sweeten and a taste sensation is revealed.

continued overleaf ⇒

Serves 6
Prep + cook time 1 hour, plus chilling

375 g (12 oz) chilled ready-made or homemade sweet shortcrust pastry
200 g (7 oz) caster sugar
40 g (1½ oz) cornflour
grated rind and juice of 2 lemons
4 eggs, separated
200–250 ml (7–8 fl oz) water

For the sauce
250 g (9 oz) sea buckthorn berries
2 teaspoons maple syrup
120g (4½ oz) granulated sugar

1. Roll out the pastry thinly on a lightly floured surface and use to line a 20 cm (8 inch) diameter x 5 cm (2 inch) deep, fluted loose-bottomed flan tin, pressing evenly into the sides. Trim the top and prick the base. Chill for 15 minutes. Line the tart with non-stick baking paper, add baking beans and bake in a preheated oven, 190°C (375°F), Gas Mark 5, for 15 minutes. Remove the paper and beans and bake for a further 5 minutes.

2. Meanwhile, put 75 g (3 oz) of the sugar in a bowl with the cornflour and lemon rind, add the egg yolks and mix until smooth. Make the lemon juice up to 300 ml (½ pint) with the measured water, pour into a saucepan and bring to the boil. Gradually mix into the yolk mixture, whisking until smooth. Pour back into the pan and bring to the boil, whisking until very thick. Pour into the pastry case and spread level.

3. Whisk the egg whites until they form stiff peaks. Gradually whisk in the remaining sugar, a teaspoonful at a time, then whisk for 1–2 minutes more until thick and glossy. Spoon over the lemon layer to cover completely and swirl with a spoon.

4. Reduce the oven temperature to 180°C (350°F), Gas Mark 4, and cook for 15–20 minutes until the meringue is golden and cooked through. Leave to stand for 15 minutes, then remove the tart tin and transfer to a serving plate.

5. Meanwhile, make the sauce. Put the berries and maple syrup in saucepan over a medium heat. Add a splash of water and bring to the boil. Turn down the heat, cover and gently simmer for 10 minutes.

6. Remove from the heat and strain through a sieve into a bowl or jug, using a spoon to push through as much of the juice and pulp as possible.

7. Return the juice to the pan, add the sugar and cook over a low heat, stirring, until the sugar has dissolved. Pour into a jug, allow to cool and serve with the pie.

Elbereth's Star-Berry Cream

Here is a sweet dish that might be made for feast-days in Valinor. Just as in the real world blueberries grow in Canada and the north-eastern United States, we may speculate that this low-lying shrub also grew in the north of Valinor, perhaps in the hills about Formenos, the 'Northern Fortress' of Fëanor and his sons. The Native Americans have gathered the sky-coloured fruit of wild blueberries for thousands of years, calling them 'star-berries' for their star-shaped blossoms. They also used blueberry root to make a tea.

We have named the cream for Varda, Queen of the Valar, who created the stars and who for this reason was especially venerated by the Elves, who first came into being under starlight. One of her titles is Elbereth, which in Sindarin means 'Queen of the Stars'. Best eaten outside on a cloudless, bright night.

———··——›

These little desserts are lovely accompanied by mini meringues or lemon shortbread. For a banana version, replaced the blueberries with 2 sliced bananas and decorate the finished desserts with a sprinkling of grated dark chocolate.

Serves 6
Prep + cook time 15 minutes,
  plus cooling

150 g (5 oz) granulated sugar

3 tablespoons cold water

2 tablespoons boiling water

150 g (5 oz) fresh (not frozen)
   blueberries

400 g (13 oz) fromage frais

425 g (14 oz) ready-made custard

1. Put the sugar and measured cold water into a frying pan and heat gently, stirring very occasionally until the sugar has completely dissolved. Bring to the boil and cook for 3–4 minutes, without stirring, until the syrup is just changing colour and is golden around the edges.

2. Add the measured boiling water, standing well back as the syrup will spit, then tilt the pan to mix. Add the blueberries and cook for 1 minute. Take the pan off the heat and set aside to cool slightly.

3. Mix the fromage frais and custard together, spoon into small dishes, then spoon the blueberry mixture over the top. Serve immediately.

Legolas's Bramble Pudding

Of all Tolkien's Elves, Legolas is the one we get to know best and the most fully rounded. For the most part the Elven characters of *The Silmarillion* – with some exceptions such as Thingol, Fëanor and Lúthien perhaps – remain somewhat remote and 'mythological'. Even in *The Lord of the Rings* the characters of Elrond, Galadriel and Arwen are Tolkien stock types (we might even say archetypes) – the wise old man, the powerful queen and the ever-patient, ever-faithful princess, respectively. Legolas, of course, is also something of an Elvish stereotype – keen-eyed, a superlative archer, somewhat haughty, in tune with nature ... but he is also a fully fleshed-out character. He even has something of a narrative arc – gaining a wider empathy for the world and its peoples as he leaves behind his native prejudices, as we see in his evolving relationship with the Dwarf Gimli.

Every well-rounded character has a backstory, too, of which the novelist can provide as much as they like and the reader can fill in as much as they choose. So we might like to think of Legolas, as Thranduil's only son, as having a rather closeted childhood, a Sindarin prince kept apart from the Elvenking's lower-born Green-elf subjects. Nonetheless he also has a rebellious streak and, come autumn, sneaks out from his father's halls to go berrying in the forest, returning with a full stomach and tell-tale purple smears around his mouth.

continued overleaf ⇒

This spin on a conventional trifle is very versatile: you can enjoy it hot in winter and it's also lovely cold in summer. For a boozy version, stir a splash of brandy or whisky into the poached fruit mixture.

Serves 4
Prep + cook time 45 minutes, plus cooling

150 g (5 oz) fresh or frozen blackberries
2 dessert apples, cored, peeled and sliced
1 tablespoon water
50 g (2 oz) caster sugar
4 trifle sponges
3 tablespoons dry or sweet sherry
425 g (14 oz) ready-made custard

For the meringue
3 egg whites
75 g (3 oz) caster sugar

1. Put the blackberries, apples, measured water and sugar in a saucepan, then cover and simmer for 5 minutes or until the fruit has softened. Leave the mixture to cool slightly.

2. Break the trifle sponges into chunks and arrange in an even layer in the base of a 1.2 litre (2 pint) ovenproof pie or soufflé dish and drizzle with the sherry. Spoon the poached fruit and syrup over the top, then cover with the custard.

3. Whisk the egg whites in a large, dry bowl until stiffly peaking, then gradually whisk in the sugar, a teaspoonful at a time, until the meringue is stiff and glossy. Spoon over the custard and swirl the top with the back of a spoon.

4. Bake in a preheated oven, 180°C (350°F), Gas Mark 4, for 15–20 minutes until heated through and the meringue is golden. Serve immediately.

Ossë's Jelly

Some of the Valar and Maia are closer to, and more sympathetic, to the Elves than others. One such is the Maia, Ossë, a servant of Ulmo, Lord of Waters, a spirit who delights in islands and seashores but who has a wild, unpredictable temperament. He has something in common with the minor Greek sea gods such as Triton, Nereus and Proteus.

During the Great Journey of the Elves west, Ossë befriends some of the Teleri Elves on the shores of the ocean and persuades some, including Círdan (page 21), to remain there, rather than travelling onward to Valinor. He teaches them all the ways of the sea – shipbuilding, navigation and sea-music, and perhaps sea-cuisine as well.

We imagine that, originally, this delicious pudding – one of Ossë's specialities – would have been set using carageen – made from the dried seaweed gathered from the wild shores of the Falas – but nowadays agar-agar will do just as well!

———

Go retro with jelly, everyone's childhood favourite. This recipe uses agar-agar, made from seaweed, rather than gelatine, making it suitable for vegans and vegetarians. Jellies made with agar-agar are much firmer than those made with gelatine, but just as delicious. Serve with raspberries or strawberries and non-dairy ice cream.

Serves 4
Prep + cook time 15 minutes,
 plus standing and setting

1 litre (1¾ pints) cranberry juice
4 tablespoons agar-agar flakes
100 g (3½ oz) caster sugar

1. Pour the cranberry juice into a saucepan and sprinkle in the agar-agar flakes and sugar. Stir, then leave to stand for 10 minutes to allow the agar-agar to soften.

2. Heat over a low heat, stirring, until the sugar has dissolved. Bring up to the boil and boil for 1–2 minutes or until the agar-agar has completely melted.

3. Take off the heat and pour into a jelly mould. Leave to cool completely, then chill in the fridge for 4 hours until set. Unmould the jelly onto a serving plate and serve.

Simbelmynë Ice Cream

As we know, Tolkien mostly drew on real-world flora and fauna for the plants and animals of Middle-earth but occasionally invented new, imagined species (page 144). One of these is simbelmynë – called by the Elves uilos or alfirin – a low-growing plant with small white flowers. In *The Silmarillion*, Tolkien records them as growing in a ravine between the Fourth and Fifth Gates on the path to the hidden Elvish city of Gondolin (see page 31). In later ages, the flower often grew on the graves of warrior Men: the name simbelmynë means 'Ever-mind', suggestive of its role as a flower of remembrance, a kind of 'forget-me-not'.

Tolkien compared the flower to the anemone, but perhaps it also has a resemblance to sweet woodruff, whose star-like, white flowers soldiers once placed inside their helmets for luck on the battlefield – a martial association shared with simbelmynë. Here we use the sweet, fragrant leaves of woodruff to make a delicious, strikingly flavoured ice cream.

Mild and sweet, woodruff – a little-known herb but one well worth growing in your herb garden – adds a delicate grassy note to this ice cream. For a tropical version, replace the woodruff with 2 star anise.

Serves 6
Prep + cook time 30 minutes, plus infusing and freezing

300 ml (½ pint) full-fat milk
400 ml (14 fl oz) can full-fat coconut milk
20g (¾ oz) sweet woodruff leaves
5 egg yolks
75 g (3 oz) caster sugar

1. Place the milk, coconut milk and woodruff in a saucepan over a low heat and bring just to the boil. Take off the heat and leave to infuse for at least 2 hours. Strain and discard the woodruff leaves.

2. In a bowl, beat the egg yolks with the caster sugar until pale and creamy. Stir in the milk mixture, then pour into a saucepan. Heat gently, stirring, until the mixture coats the back of a spoon. Take off the heat and allow to cool.

3. Pour into an ice cream maker and process according to the manufacturer's instructions or pour into a freezer-proof container. Place in the freezer until the edges start to freeze then remove from the freezer and beat the ice cream vigorously with a fork or electric hand mixer. Return to the freezer and repeat this step at least twice (breaking up the mixture will make your ice cream smooth and creamy), then leave to freeze until ready to serve.

A Botanical Treasure Trove

Tolkien loved nature. As a child he learned botany from his mother and liked nothing better than to ramble through the countryside about his Midlands home, getting to know its plants and flowers. He transposed this love into his writing: when reading *The Lord of the Rings*, as we follow the progress of his characters through the vast and varied landscapes of Middle-earth we, too, become immersed in its natural world. We feel the rich earth underfoot in The Shire, we become entangled in the brambles and nettles of the Old Forest, and we gaze across to the haze of the Misty Mountains on the far horizon. We experience every kind of weather, too – from the unsparing rains that seep through the seams of the travellers' clothes, to the knuckle-blistering blizzards on Mount Caradhras, to the scorching sunshine of southern lands like Gondor.

The reader's imaginative immersion in nature is made possible by Tolkien's meticulous and deeply empathic descriptions of the living landscapes of his continent and the trees, plants and herbs that flourish there. Nature, in *The Lord of the Rings* especially, is as much a character as the Hobbits, Men and Elves who live and depend on it. There is plenty of luminous detail – from the smooth silver-grey bark of the mallorn trees of Lothlórien; to the long, pungent leaves of athelas, or Kingsfoil, used to treat Frodo's Morgul knife wound; to the brakes of old brown fern that Frodo and Sam bed down in the shadows of the mountains of Mordor. Nature feels inhabited – literally so in the case of the Ents, Tolkien's walking trees.

In *The Two Towers*, the Ent Treebeard tells the Hobbits Merry and Pippin about the disappearance of the Entwives, a sad tale told in the songs of Elves and Men. The Ents – a name Tolkien borrowed from the Anglo-Saxon word for 'giants' – concerned themselves with shepherding the wild trees of Middle-earth's forests and woods, and were taught to speak with them by the Elves. The Entwives, however, were increasingly drawn to the 'lesser' trees – such as the wild cherry and wild apple – domesticating them in their orchards and gardens. The Entwives – who to some extent resemble the helpful Dryads (wood-nymphs) of Greek mythology – taught the horticultural arts to Men and also, we assume, to the Elves.

Mostly based on the real-world species of Northern Europe, the botany of Middle-earth is enriched with species more or less invented, sometimes supernatural – many, like the mallorn and athelas, introduced from Aman or Númenor. Tolkien was also careful to vary his flora from region to region, land to land, so that, for example, each of his forests or woodlands are distinctive from the others. Lothlórien and Fangorn are only a few dozen miles from each other but are entirely different as biomes: the former spacious and bright and full of flowers – the white-flowered niphredil and the golden star-shaped elanor – and the latter dim, musty, cramped – like the Old Took's study, Pippin comments.

How this botanical richness and variety shaped the Elves' culinary heritage we can only guess. To some extent, there would have been staples grown regardless of place or time – the corn grown to make the Elvish waybread; orchard fruits like apples and plums; kitchen gardens of vegetables of much the same kind we find in The Shire – carrots, cabbages, potatoes and so forth – but these would have been supplemented by more local species and varieties, foraged and gathered, herbs, roots, nuts, mushrooms and berries.

Drinks

E lves drink for all the reasons humans do – to quench their thirst, for refreshment, to celebrate and make merry, and perhaps even on occasion to get drunk and forget their worries and woes. There are even hints that in certain circumstances a drink can have a spiritual significance, just as the Elvish waybread lembas does.

Of non-alcoholic drinks miruvor is the most quintessentially Elvish – a cordial or tonic that made its appearance very early on in the evolution of Tolkien's legendarium. Golden-coloured and invigorating, it might be described as magical, though the Elves themselves would be dismissive of that word. For them, everything in nature derives ultimately from Eru Ilúvatar, the All-Father.

Among alcoholic drinks, wine is clearly the drink of choice for the Elves, although every people in Middle-earth – Hobbits, Men, Dwarves and no doubt Orcs – seems to enjoy a glass or two. The Elves appear to have developed viticulture in the First Age (they may well have learned it from the Valar), and by the Third Age wine is produced and enjoyed in every corner of the continent, from The Shire to Gondor to Rhovanion. Few seem to be such a wine connoisseur, though, as the Elvenking of Greenwood, whose cellars are lined with barrels of the best vintages and who even has a butler-cum-sommelier to take care of them!

Here you will find choice drinks for every occasion – from two versions of miruvor through a home-made sloe gin to a heady wine punch of which even the Elvenking would have approved.

Gildor's Elderflower Cordial

Soon after the three Hobbit companions – Frodo, Pippin and Sam – leave the High Elves at Woody End (page 41), they discover that their hosts have thoughtfully filled their water bottles with a delicious drink. Tolkien does not identify the drink – presumably because the Hobbits cannot know what it is – but it does have strong similarities with the revitalizing drink miruvor (page 147) that turns up quite often in the legendarium.

Tolkien describes the cordial's appearance ('pale golden'), scent (like 'honey made of many flowers') and effects ('wonderfully refreshing') in some detail; it even seems to lift the Hobbits' mood, causing them to laugh and flick their finger at the rain, though without inebriating them. Perhaps we wouldn't expect anything less of an Elvish drink – the perfect stimulant without side-effects or a hangover.

We might conjecture that miruvor – named for the nectar-drink of the Valar, miruvórë – is the exiled Elves' attempt to recreate the elixirs they drank in Valinor and that they make it in different versions, with whatever ingredients are close to hand. Our version of Gildor's cordial here, then, is made from elderflowers, which would have grown abundantly in the woodlands of The Shire.

⌐—···—⌐

The creamy white flowers of the elder tree make a great cordial. Gather them on dry day and, before you add them to the cordial, fill a large bowl with cold water and gently swish the elderflower heads in it to get rid of any dirt or insects. You can buy citric acid at chemists, some supermarkets and online.

Makes about 1 litre (1¾ pints)
Prep time 10 minutes, plus
standing

20 elderflower heads
3 lemons, sliced
25 g (1 oz) citric acid
1 kg (2 lb) granulated or caster sugar
1 litre (1¾ pints) boiling water

1. Put the elderflower heads, sliced lemons and citric acid in a large heatproof bowl. Dissolve the sugar in the measured boiling water, stirring frequently until dissolved.

2. Add to the bowl of elderflowers. Cover and leave to stand overnight. Strain through a muslin-lined sieve and pour into sterilized bottles. Store in a cool place and use within 6 months.

Cordial of Imladris

Here is another version of miruvor, this one inspired by the Cordial of Imladris entrusted by Elrond to Gandalf when the Fellowship of the Ring leaves Rivendell (Imladris in Sindarin). Elrond's cordial is clearly more precious and more potent than Gildor's, since he bestows only a single bottle, whereas, back in the Shire, Gildor liberally filled all three Hobbits' bottles. The Hobbits quaffed back the drink rather cavalierly, it seems, while Gandalf produces Elrond's cordial only in extremis, when the Fellowship are struggling through blizzards on Mount Caradhras. Indeed, he tells his companions that the drink is 'very precious' and allows them only a mouthful each, enough, though, to renew their strength and resolve.

—•••—

For a refreshing drink, dilute the cordial with water in a ratio of 1:3, adding a few of the sliced lemons for decoration, plus ice cubes and sprigs of fresh mint or lemon balm. And, if serving to adults, you might like to add a splash of vodka or gin.

Makes about 20 glasses
Prep + cook time 20 minutes,
   plus cooling

3 unwaxed lemons, washed and very
   thinly sliced
2 tablespoons honey
100 g (3½ oz) fresh root ginger,
   peeled and thinly sliced
625 g (1¼ lb) granulated sugar
900 ml (1½ pints) water
25 g (1 oz) tartaric acid

1. Add the lemon slices, honey, ginger, sugar and measured water to a saucepan, bring to the boil and then simmer over a low heat for about 20 minutes, stirring occasionally, until the sugar has dissolved and the lemons are almost translucent. Remove from the heat and stir in the tartaric acid. Leave to cool.

2. Remove some of the lemon slices using a slotted spoon and set aside. Strain the cordial into sterilized, wide-necked bottles or storage jars and add the reserved lemon slices. Seal well and store in the refrigerator for up to 1 month.

Elanor & Lissuin Iced Tea

The majority of the flora and fauna that Tolkien describes as flourishing in Middle-earth derive from real-world species. As we traipse around woodlands and fields with the Hobbits in The Shire, as Tolkien describes the stands of oak and beech or the tangled masses of nettles, cow-parsley and brambles, we may well feel ourselves very much at home. The author was a very fine nature writer.

For the landscapes of the Elves, Tolkien occasionally introduced invented, or half-invented, species. Notably in Lothlórien we find the mallorn – massive, beech-like trees that shed their golden autumn leaves only in spring, to make way for the new growth. Likewise in Lothlórien, we find the gold-and-silver star-shaped flower elanor, which Tolkien compared to a slightly oversized pimpernel. Another flower beloved of the Elves was the fragrant lissuin, which originally grew on Tol Eressëa (see page 45).

For this cool refreshing drink we have brought together elanor and lissuin to make a refreshing drink strangely reminiscent of the old British recipe dandelion and burdock. Laze away an afternoon sipping this, on a hammock suspended between mallorn trees.

―·‥·―

Packed with antioxidants, this health-boosting iced tea is a great choice for any time of day. For an after-dinner drink to aid digestion, serve with sprigs of fresh mint or, for a citrus tang, serve with slices of lemon or orange. You can stir in some honey while the tea is still warm if you'd like it a little sweeter.

Makes 850 ml (1½ pints)
Prep + cook 15 minutes plus steeping

1 tablespoon dried dandelion root
1 tablespoon dried burdock root
850 ml (1½ pints) water
ice cubes

1. Put the dandelion and burdock root and the measured water in a saucepan over a medium heat and bring to the boil. Turn down the heat and simmer the tea for 10 minutes. Take off the heat and allow to cool.

2. Strain the tea into a jug or clean bottle. To serve, pour over ice cubes in a tall glass. The tea can be stored in the fridge for up to 1 week.

Goldberry's Nettle Tisane

Tolkien describes nettles, along with hemlock, thistles and wood-parsley, growing rampantly in the Bonfire Glade of the Old Forest – the clearing where the Brandybuck Hobbit clan once cut down and burned hundreds of trees in a counter-attack against the forest after it assailed the High Hay, the dense hedge grown to protect Buckland. Frodo and his companions have now left the Shire and it is the beginning of the autumn, and the author paints a rather dismal picture of the clearing in which these wasteland weeds have grown unchecked and are now going to seed.

There's no doubt, though, that Tom Bombadil and his wife, Goldberry – whom the Hobbits are about to meet and who are practised foragers, it seems, if their meals are anything to go by – make good use of the nettle, which makes a good soup or, as here, a soothing, fresh-tasting tisane.

The nature of Goldberry, the 'River-woman's daughter', is much debated – is she a Maia (a lesser spirit and servant of the Valar) or is she something altogether different, a personification of fruitful nature, as Tolkien seems to hint? Whatever her origins, garbed in silver-green and flower-like, she has the appearance of the Elven queens who abound in European mythologies as well as in Tolkien's legendarium.

Wear rubber gloves to gather the nettle leaves you need for this refreshing tisane. Look for older nettle leaves, as these will taste slightly sweeter (older nettle leaves tend to be longer and less heart-shaped than younger ones). Wash the nettles thoroughly before using them.

Serves 4
Prep + cook time 20 minutes

50 g (2 oz) nettle leaves, roughly
    chopped
1 litre (1¾ pints) water
1 tablespoon sugar or honey, plus extra
    to taste (optional)

1. Put the nettles in a large saucepan with the measured water and sugar or honey, bring to the boil and leave to simmer for about 15 minutes.

2. Strain and pour into mugs, adding more sugar or honey to taste, if liked.

Lórien's Camomile Tisane

In Tolkien's legendarium, Lórien is a vast garden with abundance of willows, flowers, fountains and lakes in Valinor – home of the husband-and-wife Valar Irmo, Master of Dreams, and Estë, the Healer. It is an Eden and Avalon all in one – both an earthly paradise and a place of rest and healing, suspended between wakefulness and sleep, reality and dream. The Elves of Valinor seek peace and rest there. Gandalf – in his 'youth' known as Olórin, as we learn in *The Lord of the Rings* – lived in Lórien for a time; his former name, appropriately, is related to the Quenya word for 'dream'.

We might imagine Olórin/Gandalf making this relaxing tisane from camomile flowers and handing it to the Elves on their arrival. Weary they may be from their troubles and sorrows, but, after drinking this, peace of mind slowly envelops them.

───··──

You'll need a juicer to make this nutrient-packed recipe. Fennel contains, among others, vitamins A, C, B6, iron, calcium and magnesium, and its aromatic liquorice flavour is perfectly complemented by the chamomile tea. If you prefer as milder flavour, replace half the fennel with lettuce leaves.

Makes about 200 ml (7 fl oz)
Prep time 5 minutes

1 lemon, plus extra to decorate
150 g (5 oz) fennel bulb
100 ml (3½ fl oz) chilled camomile tea
ice cubes

1. Roughly peel the lemon and juice it with the fennel. Mix the juice with the chilled camomile tea.

2. Pour the combined juice and tea into a glass over ice and serve with slices of lemon, to decorate.

Eöl's Sloe Gin

We know that blackthorn grows in The Shire – Bilbo has composed a walking song mentioning its sharp, ink-black fruits (sloes) that Frodo, Pippin and Sam sing as they make their way under the trees at Woody End. No doubt the trees grew widely throughout Middle-earth and probably in Beleriand, too, so we can imagine that the Elves gathered the fruits as well and put them to good use.

We have named our sloe gin for Eöl, who ruled the small, sunless woodland kingdom of Nan Elmoth, a few leagues east of his kinsman Thingol's realm, Doriath (see page 46). The Elves are complex beings, rarely portrayed as entirely good, but Eöl's temperament is far darker than his peers and his associations are always with blackness and darkness. He has dark eyes (most Elves have grey or blue eyes), is unusually friendly with the Dwarves, a people of the underground, and, himself a master-swordsmith, is the inventor of a hard, jet-black metal known as galvorn.

This is a drink that Eöl might have a sipped after a long night at his forge, nursing his bitterness and silently plotting revenge.

Tart, but full of rich body and fruity flavour, sloe gin is the ideal winter warmer drunk neat, preferably in front of a roaring fire. To enjoy on a summer evening in the garden, top it with soda or tonic water or, for a special aperitif, with prosecco.

Makes 750 ml (26 fl oz)
Prep time 15 minutes, plus storage

500 g (1 lb) sloe berries
250 g (8 oz) caster sugar
700 ml (1¼ pints) gin

1. Rinse and remove and stems on the sloes and pat them dry with a paper towel. Using a cocktail stick, prick the sloes and place them in a sterilized glass jar large enough to hold the gin.

2. Add the sugar and the gin to the jar and make sure it is securely sealed before giving the jar a good shake. Over the next week, make sure to shake the jar well once a day. Then store the jar in a cool, dark place and leave for 2–3 months.

3. Strain the gin through a sieve lined with muslin into a bowl, then pour it into a sterilized bottle.

A Laiquendi Cocktail

Of all Tolkien's kindreds of Elves the Laiquendi – the Green-elves – perhaps come closest to the conception of elves found in English folklore: secretive woodland spirits who dress in green and who are famed for their singing. In Tolkien's tales, the Laiquendi are a group of Telerin Elves who settle in the woodlands of Ossiriand, the Land of the Seven Rivers, and who largely keep themselves apart from the rest of the Elves of Beleriand. They are masters of woodlore, using stout wooden bows to hunt and fight, and knowing the usages of the hundreds of herbs and flowers that grow in their lands.

Perhaps the Laiquendi distilled something like the French liqueur Chartreuse – made with '130 herbs, plants and flowers'. Certainly, they would have loved its intense colour – green as the leaves of a summer-crowned oak tree.

Naturally a bright green colour from all the plants it contains, Green Chartreuse has a sweet, spicy, herby flavour. Its sweetness makes it the perfect foil for gin and, mixed here with vermouth, it creates a very grown-up cocktail.

Serves 1
Prep time 5 minutes

1½ measures gin
1 measure sweet vermouth
½ measure Green Chartreuse
1 dash orange bitters
ice cubes, to serve
cocktail cherry, to decorate

1. Add all of the ingredients to a cocktail shaker or mixing glass, and fill with ice cubes. Stir for 30 seconds, and strain into a chilled martini glass. Decorate with a cocktail cherry.

The Elvenking's Red Wine Punch

In *The Hobbit* the Elvenking's and the Wood-elves' partiality for red wine is an important plot point – not only does the wine make the king's guards drowsy enough for Bilbo to steal the prison keys and free his companions from their prison but the barrels that are used to transport the wine from Lake-town up the Forest River to the Elvenking's halls become the means for Bilbo and the Dwarves to smuggle themselves out of the Elvish kingdom.

The rich heady red wines most often enjoyed at the Elvenking's tables come from Dorwinion, a land on the north-western shores of the Sea of Rhûn, far to the east of Mirkwood. For the Elvenking's punch here – perfect for an al fresco lunch in a forest glade – we recommend a rather lighter wine.

Celebrate balmy summer days with this punch. Its fruity, light and delicious, quick to prep and perfect when entertaining a crowd. You can vary the fruit you include, depending on what's in season, but opt for ones that won't disintegrate while sitting in the jug.

Serves 10
Prep time 5 minutes, plus chilling

20–30 ice cubes
2 x 750 ml (1¼ pints) bottles light
   Spanish red wine, chilled
125 ml (4 fl oz) brandy (optional)
450 ml (¾ pint) soda water, chilled
slices of fruit such as apples, pears,
   oranges, lemons, peaches and
   strawberries
slices of orange, to decorate

1. Put the ice in a large serving jug, and pour over the wine and brandy, if using. Give everything a stir.

2. Add the soda water and the slices of fruit. If you are making it ahead, add the soda water at the last minute.

3. To serve, decorate the side of each glass with an orange slice and pour in the sangria.

Index

Picture Acknowledgements

Victor Ambrus: front cover, 3, 7, 14, 21, 25, 42, 58, 79, 89, 96, 111, 114, 124, 128, 155; **Allan Curless:** 139; **Andrew Mockett:** front cover; **Octopus Publishing Group:** Stephen Conroy 30, 33, 91, 127, 136, 156; Will Heap 37, 47, 133, 141; Lis Parsons 49, 63, 65, 98, 107, 153; William Reavell 57; Craig Roberts 95; William Shaw 17, 22, 27, 54, 75, 81, 87, 113; Ian Wallace 105, 117; **iStock** (used throughout and on cover): Alhontess, Andrea_Hill, ant_art, bombuscreative, ilbusca, Jon Wightman, Kseniia Gorova, Nastasic, Neil Hubert, Neuevector, smartboy10.